A Library of Lemons

Jo Cotterill

Piccadilly
PRESS

First published in the UK in 2016
by Piccadilly Press
80–81 Wimpole St, London W1G 9RE
www.piccadillypress.co.uk

A CIP catalogue record for this book is available
from the British Library

ISBN: 978-1-848-12511-7
Also available as an ebook

3 5 7 9 10 8 6 4

Typeset in Sabon 12/17.5 pt by
Palimpsest Book Production Limited, Falkirk, Stirlingshire

Printed in the UK by Clays Ltd, St Ives Plc

For all my friends over the years,
but particularly Shelley and Mandie,
Claire, Esther, John, Cas,
Helen and Steve.

And Phil, the best.

1

The new girl, Mae, asked me to play with her today. I didn't know what to say. She's got long black hair that she'd tied into two plaits and put on top of her head, like Heidi or the children from *The Sound of Music.* She has a round doll face with bright blue eyes, and she only joined the school this term.

I was sitting in my favourite corner of the playground, with a book. It's what I always do at break-time. Mae smiled at me in a hopeful way, but I shook my head and went back to my book.

'Okay,' she said, and went.

I tried to concentrate on my book, but my eyes kept sliding over to watch her. She says okay a lot; it seems to suit her. It even rhymes with her name. Okay, Mae. She told us in circle time she'd changed schools because her family had moved house. She didn't seem to mind about it, though. She always looked cheerful.

I thought maybe she would go up to someone else but she went over to the fence on her own and started to pick up twigs from the ground. She made a little pile of them. Then she sat down and pulled something out of her pocket. The sun glinted off it – a magnifying glass.

She was trying to set fire to the twigs. I watched, fascinated. Would it work? She seemed to be having difficulty getting the angle right. She kept looking up at the sky and then down at the magnifying glass, tilting it from side to side.

That's not right, I thought to myself. She needs to hold it in one position for a long time, so that the pinpoint of light heats up the twig underneath. I read it in a book once. Lighting a fire that way isn't actually very practical, but it can work if you're patient enough and if the sun is strong enough. But this is autumn. The sun isn't very strong.

I was watching her so hard that when she looked up and saw me, I nearly dropped my book in shock. Quickly, I fixed my eyes on the page again, but I couldn't resist sneaking another glance at her. She was still looking at me, and she smiled as if I was her friend.

My face felt hot with embarrassment. I didn't look up from my book again.

Mae didn't manage to set fire to her twigs. I know that because if she had, one of the teachers would have come running. Instead, when the bell went, everyone lined up just as normal. I dawdled behind, waiting until the line had almost gone in. Then I rushed over to the fence to look at Mae's little pile of twigs.

It wasn't a pile any more. She'd arranged them into letter shapes on the ground. They spelled out a word.

CALYPSO

I raced back to the classroom, my heart pounding. Why had she written my name in twigs?

Dad always says you should be your own best friend. When I was younger I didn't understand what that meant, but now I do. It means that you should be happy being alone, with yourself; that you shouldn't need other people to make you happy. He doesn't need other people, he says.

I wonder sometimes if he needed my mother, but it's not the sort of thing I can ask him. And I can't ask her because she's dead.

Teachers at school used to worry that I always sit by myself. They wrote things like 'she is a very solitary girl' and 'she isolates herself'. As though those were bad things.

My latest report says something different: 'She will find it hard to transition to secondary school next year if she can't form close friendships.'

'They don't get it,' Dad said when he read it at the end of last term. 'They don't understand people who don't need people. They think being independent means you must be lonely. They've never been taught about inner strength.'

Dad's a big believer in inner strength. 'If something happened to me,' Dad says every now and then, 'you'd be fine, Calypso. You have great inner strength.'

I feel proud that he thinks I have great inner strength, but I don't like to think about something happening to Dad. Something happened to Mum, five years ago, and I try not to think about that either. It all happened so quickly: she felt a bit unwell and went to the doctor, and they did some tests and told her she had cancer, and then she got very ill very fast – and then she died. If Dad died too, I'm not at all sure I'd be fine.

Whenever he says it, I feel my eyes fill with tears. He notices and shakes his head, as though I've let him down again. 'It's no good getting upset,' he says. 'I'm just showing you how to be strong. Find your inner strength.'

I wipe my eyes and try. It's there, I'm sure. He says it often enough, it must be there. 'I'd be fine,' I say, and I don't let my voice wobble. 'And if . . . something happened to me . . . *you'd* be fine.'

'That's right,' he says, with an encouraging smile, and goes off to his library. I try not to mind that he agrees. It's because he's got inner strength. It's not that he doesn't love me.

At school, the other children have stopped trying to be my best friend. I like playing with them – it's not that I don't like people. But to be honest, I prefer books. I like the quiet space in my head that they make; the space that can be filled with magic or islands or mystery.

Mae is new and doesn't understand about me yet. She'll realise in a few days, and then she'll find someone else to be her friend.

2

I'm still puzzling over Mae and her sticks when I get home. I let myself into the house and tiptoe past the library door so that I don't disturb Dad while he's working. It's a big wooden door on the left, thick and old, and probably he wouldn't hear me anyway, but I've got into the habit of being quiet. Then I go up the stairs to my bedroom and start my homework.

The library has always been Dad's work room. Mum had a little studio upstairs in the third bedroom, the smallest one. After she died, we turned it into a library for me, so now I have a bedroom *and* a library, which makes me very lucky because I don't know anyone else my age who has a whole room for their books. When Mum was alive, it was full of canvases and easels and oil paints and water-colours and brushes and white spirit. It still smells very faintly of oil paints, even though there haven't been any here for years. I like that I can sit in my library, with its walls of shelves and books, and breathe in the memory of Mum while I'm reading. It's my special place, and Dad never comes in.

After I finish my homework, I go downstairs to make tea. There isn't much in the cupboard, as usual, but there's some bread and cheese – and a tin of baked beans. I toast the bread and warm up the beans and then grate some cheese over the top. Then I sit at the kitchen table and eat with one hand – the other hand holding a book open in front of me. It's *Pollyanna*, a book from years and years ago. I'm not getting on with it very well because the heroine is astonishingly dull and wants nothing more than for everyone to like her. I'm starting to wonder whether it's worth going on with. Anne in *Anne of Green Gables* is much more my sort of character. Or Sophie in *Rooftoppers* or Louie in *The Girl Who Walked On Air*. They all have imaginations and want adventures. They don't spend their time being 'glad' about stuff.

Dad still hasn't appeared after I've finished and washed up, so I make a cup of tea for him and take it to his library.

'Dad?' I knock on the heavy door and then push it open.

Dad's desk is to the left. He's sitting there as usual, eyes glued to a manuscript. He's a proofreader, which means he reads books before they're ready to be printed, to make sure they're perfect. Dad can spot mistakes that ten editors have missed. Even nowadays, with all the computers we have, no one can beat my dad for proofreading. He does have a computer, but he hardly ever uses it. He says it's impossible to spot errors properly on a screen, so he prints out each manuscript and the desk is always covered in neat piles of paper.

The large rectangular room is quite gloomy. The trees in the front garden have grown so much that they block the light that should stream in through the big bay window – and today is overcast anyway. At some point, years before we moved in, someone knocked a hole in the wall and added a glass door to a sort of conservatory-greenhouse thing. Maybe at that point they were worried about their books being damaged by sunlight, because they also built big carved shutters to cover the beautiful old wooden shelves that line three of the walls. The sunlight doesn't reach the shelves these days, but the shutters are still always closed out of habit. Dad has to use a lamp on his desk, but he likes it that way. I do too. The library feels quiet and dark and comforting. Sometimes I imagine the characters in the books tiptoeing around behind their shutters.

'Cup of tea,' I say, and put it down on the corner of the desk.

'End of page,' he says, holding up a finger and not taking his eyes off the paper.

I wait. Dad is forty-two, but no one ever guesses his age right. He's got one of those faces that could be much younger or much older, depending on how he's feeling or what he's concentrating on at the time. His hair is sort of springy and brown, and it's slowly moving back from his forehead like the tide going out. He wears glasses for reading, and he's naturally tall, thin and gangly. Once, when I was very small, he dressed up as a scarecrow, and somehow he looked exactly right, as though he'd been one in a former life.

He reaches the bottom of the page and makes a tiny scrawl under a word on the last line. Then he looks up and smiles at me, his eyes crinkling at the corners. 'Good afternoon, Calypso. How was school?'

'Fine. The new girl made my name out of twigs on the ground.'

He takes off his glasses and tilts his head to one side. 'Strange.'

'Yes, I know.'

'Were you playing a game with her?'

'No, she just did it.'

'Did she make her own name?'

'No, just mine.'

He shrugs. 'Ah well. People do odd things sometimes.'

'I know. What are you working on?'

His face brightens. 'A scientific journal. There's a particularly good article about citric acid. I'm thinking of asking the author to review my History when it's out.'

Dad is writing what he calls his '*magnum opus*', which sounds like an ice cream but is actually a really big book. It's called *A History of the Lemon* and it's all about where lemons originated, how they've developed over the centuries, what medicines can be made with lemons, recipes . . . everything to do with the lemon, really. I think it's great that one day he's going to be a famous author. Sometimes, when I'm in my library, surrounded by books and the people who wrote them, I secretly dream of becoming an author myself. It's not something I've dared to say out loud though, in case that somehow spoils it, like a bubble popping when you breathe on it.

Dad's library used to smell of beeswax polish, but now it smells of lemons because he's growing his own trees. Four years ago he cleared out the conservatory-greenhouse thing with a kind of mad enthusiasm. Then he bought six lemon trees at the garden centre and a book about how to look after them. That was a very strange day. I went to school in the morning, and when I came back there was a lemon orchard in the house. I think it was soon after that he started writing his book.

I tried reading to the trees once, because I'd heard that plants like to be read to. Dad asked me to stop after one of them developed brown leaves.

'You will remember to eat dinner, won't you, Dad?' I ask now.

'Dinner?' He looks puzzled.

'Yes. Do you want me to make you some toast? I'm afraid I had the last tin of beans.'

'What time is it?'

'Half past six.'

'Half past six, already?' he says. 'You're late home from school.'

'I've been home for hours, Dad.'

'Have you? I didn't hear you come in.'

'Dinner, Dad,' I say patiently.

'Oh, I don't fancy toast.'

'Okay . . . well, there's not much else.'

He frowns. 'You know I don't like that word, Calypso. Please don't use it.'

'Sorry.'

Dad claims that the word 'okay' is common and slang and not good English, but it's hard to remember when everyone at school uses it all the time. And it's Mae's favourite word too. Okay, Mae. She's a nice sort of person – isn't it okay for people to say okay? I open my mouth to ask Dad whether it's okay for some people to use the word and not others and, if so, how you know which sort of person you are, but his head suddenly jerks up and he fixes me with a delighted stare, the frown wiped from his forehead.

'Shall we go out for pizza?'

If anyone looked at him now, they'd never know he was in his forties. He looks like a big excited kid.

I blink. 'What, now?'

‘Of course!’ He jumps up and runs a hand through his scrubby hair. ‘Let’s be spontaneous!’

‘I just had beans, Dad.’

‘But you can still fit in pizza, can’t you? Everyone loves pizza. Get your coat!’

‘I was going to have a bath . . .’ But it’s no use. He’s already in the hallway, trying to find his shoes.

I slip my book into my jacket pocket and follow him.

Our wheezy Volkswagen almost doesn’t start, and I hold my breath.

‘Come on, old girl,’ Dad says. ‘Easy does it.’

It strikes me that in some ways Dad is like a character from *Pollyanna*. Surely no one calls their car ‘old girl’ these days?

The car coughs into life and I breathe with relief. Some day, and it can’t be that far off, the car won’t start at all. Cars are supposed to be serviced, I know that. But I don’t think ours has been serviced in years. It’s probably a ‘menace to society’, which is what Mrs Gilkes, our head teacher, calls anyone and anything she disapproves of.

Dad eats a lot of pizza. I’m still full of toast and beans, so I only have a couple of slices, but it’s nice.

I wish Dad had suggested it earlier, though, because then I could have saved the beans for tomorrow.

'We need to get some food in,' I say to Dad as we come out of the restaurant.

He nods. 'I'll do it while you're at school.'

'Really? You won't forget like last time?'

He grins and takes my hand as we walk to the car. 'Scout's honour.'

I feel happy. In bed I read another chapter of *Pollyanna* and frown. What is calf's-foot jelly? It doesn't sound very nice.

I reach out and brush my fingers against the photo frame that stands on my bedside table, the way I always do before I go to sleep. 'Goodnight, Mum,' I say.

She smiles back at me from the frame, her long auburn hair lit up by sunlight. I don't know if the sun really shone more when I was little, but it feels that way.

Then I turn off the lamp and think about Mae. She's a bit like Pollyanna. A cheerful sort of person. I wonder if she'll try to make friends with me again tomorrow.

I'm not sure if I want her to or not.

3

Miss Spotlin pairs up me and Mae on a writing activity. We have to match words together that mean the same thing. I know Miss Spotlin has given us the advanced vocab envelope, because the words are printed in purple. Most of the class have green or blue words. The dyslexic group is given red ones.

I know a lot of words because I read a lot. Being paired with Mae makes me wonder if she reads a lot too. Or maybe Miss Spotlin didn't know where else to put her.

'Talkative,' I say, reaching for a word, 'and loquacious.'

Mae nods. 'Worried,' she says, matching it to 'anxious'.

That was an easy pair.

'Sophistication and elegance,' I say.

Mae says, 'Volatile and explosive.'

I am impressed. Not many people in my class know what 'volatile' means. Maybe Mae does read lots of books. My eyes scan the little white rectangles for more matches.

Mae beats me to it. 'Minuscule and diminutive.'

I raise my eyebrows and reach for 'cerebral' and 'intellectual'.

'You're good at this,' Mae says to me.

'So are you,' I reply.

She beams. 'I like words.'

'Me too.' I feel something approaching surprise. I've never met anyone my own age who would admit to 'liking words'.

'Words are kind of like food, don't you think?' she says, her eyes on the printed strips. 'They have flavours, and they all feel different in your mouth. I mean, even though "cerebral" and "intellectual" mean the same thing, they feel different. "Cerebral" is almost slinky, or sugary – the end of the word makes it feel like it's almost falling out of your mouth. And "intellectual" is kind of like a marching rhythm. In-tel-lec-tual. It's sort of chewy with a snap.'

I'm not quite sure what to say because I've never thought about words that way before, and now my brain is sort of sputtering in response to the idea and no sentences come out.

We match all the rest of the pairs in record time. Miss Spotlin laughs when we call her over. 'I haven't got a harder pack,' she says regretfully. 'You'll have to do some reading.'

Mae seems pleased at this. She and I both go to our drawers and pull out a book. I have given up on *Pollyanna* because I had a horrible dream about being forced to eat calf's-foot jelly and it made me feel sick. Now I'm trying *Black Beauty*, which is a story about a horse, but not a warm, fuzzy story. It's set in the olden days, and Black Beauty is treated badly by several people. I don't much like horses, but the story is good, even if the sentences are a bit too long sometimes. After what Mae said, though, I have this great urge to read the words out loud to see how they feel in my mouth.

Instead, I sneak a glance at Mae's book. She's reading something called *The Diary of a Young Girl*.

'A diary?' I ask, and I don't mean to sound suspicious but my voice comes out that way. The only diary book I've ever read was about a girl who discovered she was really a princess and I thought it was a bit silly. 'What kind of diary?'

'It's about the war,' said Mae. 'The girl in the story – Anne, her name is – had to hide away from the Nazis.'

I know about the Nazis. I read a book about a German boy who made friends with a Jewish boy in a concentration camp run by Nazis. It was a very disturbing story.

'Who wrote the book?' I ask.

'She did. The girl – Anne. It's not made up, it's a true story. She's really famous now.'

'She published her own diary?'

'No,' says Mae. 'She died.'

I am baffled. 'Then how come you're reading her diary?'

'Her father found it, after the war.' Mae's eyes fill with tears. 'It's so sad, Calypso. She died just before the war ended. If she'd only hung on a bit longer . . .' She sniffs and wipes her eyes. 'Anyway, it's really good. You should read it.'

'Maybe I will,' I say, captivated now. I show her my own book. 'I'm reading this.'

'Oh, I love *Black Beauty*!' Mae exclaims. 'But poor Ginger!'

'What happens to Ginger?'

She claps her hand to her mouth. 'Oh, I'm so sorry! I shouldn't have said anything! You haven't got to that bit yet.'

'Got to what bit?'

'I can't tell you! I can't tell you!' She looks almost manic now. 'Oh, I hate it when someone spoils a book for me! I'm so sorry! Please forgive me!'

'Of course I forgive you,' I say, slightly alarmed by her fervour. And also now wondering what on earth happens to Ginger. I hope this book doesn't give me bad dreams too.

She heaves a sigh of relief. 'Thank goodness. I won't say another word, I promise.' She zips her mouth shut with a gesture. Then she unzips it again to say, 'I knew we'd like the same kinds of books. I saw you reading *Pollyanna* yesterday. Hasn't she got a beautiful name? *Pollyanna*. Like . . . *lollipop*. Or *crystalline*. They feel so delicious to say. I'd love to have a pretty name, like yours. *Calypso*. How amazing to be named after music!'

'Oh,' I say, unsure how to respond.

'That's why I made your name in twigs, because I like it so much and I wanted to write it on the ground.'

'Well . . . thank you. I like your name too,' I say, feeling this is probably the right sort of thing to say in return. 'It's kind of . . . summery. Or hopeful. You know. Dreams *may* come true.'

She stares at me with her big eyes. 'Oh,' she breathes. 'That's so lovely. That helps me like it more. Thank you.'

I look down, slightly embarrassed. 'I didn't finish *Pollyanna*, I'm afraid. I . . . er . . . had a bad dream about calf's-foot jelly.'

Mae's little nose wrinkles nicely. 'Ew, it sounds horrible, doesn't it? I looked it up. It's basically jelly made from boiling baby cows' feet. But you know jelly in the shops is actually made with it, don't you?'

'Is it?' My jaw drops. 'You're joking.'

'I'm not. It's called gelatine.'

I shudder. 'I wish I'd never even started the book.'

'Oh, it's a shame you didn't get to the end,' says Mae. 'The ending made me cry! But then,' she adds, 'I cry at the end of most books. Don't you?'

'N-no, not really.'

There's a pause.

'Oh – just me then.' She gives me an uncertain smile, and the conversation stops, just like that.

After a pause, we both start reading our books again.

I feel odd, and a bit upset, like I've made a mistake, but I'm not sure what it is or how to put it right.

4

At home, I stare at the contents of the fridge. Dad has forgotten to go shopping again. We have half a block of cheese, two out-of-date yoghurts and a jar of pickled onions. The bread is going mouldy, but there are a few greenish potatoes. Cheese and onion and potato go together, don't they? I could boil up the potatoes and mash everything together. It might taste nice.

All of a sudden I feel very tired, like something is pressing down on my head and shoulders. I don't want to think about cooking supper. I overhear other children sometimes in the playground, talking about food at their houses. They have roast chicken with potatoes and carrots and beans and gravy – and they don't have to make any of it themselves. They can carry on playing or watching TV or whatever they do, while their mums or dads cook the dinner. Scarlett Callahan says she never even has to empty the dishwasher or washing machine. Her mum does it all! That reminds me – I don't have any clean socks for tomorrow. I should put a wash on, but I can't bear to drag myself upstairs to collect the laundry and scrabble around on the floor of Dad's room for the clothes he never remembers to put in the basket.

I sit down on a kitchen chair and stare at the table. The surface is scratched and dented from meals over the years. There are several sticky patches of jam or honey. I should get a cloth and wipe the table – it would only take a minute. But somehow I can't persuade my legs to move or my arms to reach for the cloth.

My mind has slowed. Why is this moment so hard? I could go up to my library. Read; breathe in the faint smell of oil paints; be comforted. But it's like I'm made of lead. What happened at school today? Mae and I . . . it feels strange to say 'Mae and I', even in my head . . . we had a conversation. A connection. And then it broke. Did I break it? I don't know. Sometimes the rules of conversation are too hard to work out. It's easier to stay silent, or alone.

I'm not sure how long I sit like that. The only sounds are the tick, tick, tick of the kitchen clock and the faint hiccupping of the fridge. I feel empty.

Then Dad wanders in and switches on the light. I blink, confused for a moment. Did I conjure him up out of a wish for company?

'Hello,' he says in surprise. 'Why are you sitting in the dark? Is everything all right?'

I bite my lip because I feel like crying and I know he wouldn't like it. I can't speak, so instead I shrug.

Dad comes and sits down. 'You look sad. Can I help with something?'

And then the tears run down my face and I can't stop my lip doing that childish quivering thing, and it feels like there's a piston in my chest heaving the sobs out.

Dad looks quite alarmed. He reaches out to pat me on the shoulder. 'Dear me, Calypso, are you ill?'

I shake my head, unable to speak.

He looks relieved. 'Oh good. Well, cheer up. I'm sure it can't be that bad.'

I want to be wrapped in his arms so I can sob into his shirt and feel safe. But his arm is outstretched, leaving space between us, and when I lean forward slightly, he moves a fraction backwards, away from me. I know he is probably trying to remind me about inner strength, but I wish so hard that he would just hug me, like I've seen other parents do when their kids are crying in the playground.

I sit on my chair, rigid and shaking, while the tears come and he pats my arm and looks worried. And I cry that bit harder because I'm angry that he can't just do this one thing for me – and then I cry because I feel guilty that I'm not strong enough to hold myself up.

After a few minutes, I get control of myself again, and Dad nods. 'Well done. Now we can talk. Shall I make a cup of tea?'

'There's no milk,' I say, and it comes out sharply.

'Isn't there? Oh!' He realises. 'I didn't go shopping. I'm sorry, Calypso. I forgot. I was reading this fascinating article online about a lemon grove in Sicily and their radical experiments with hybrid plants.'

I don't care, I want to say. You didn't go shopping and you promised you would. You said Scout's honour. And I'm trying so hard to find inner strength but I'm not sure where to look.

'It doesn't matter,' I say. 'I'm just not sure what to have for supper and I'm a bit hungry.'

Dad leans forward and smiles at me. 'Well, we can't have that. Let's see what I can do about it.' He gets to his feet and starts opening cupboards. 'Hmm, not much in here, is there? Ah! Pasta! And . . . hmmm . . .' Packets and boxes appear on the table, most of them nearly empty. 'We should have a proper clear-out, shouldn't we?'

'I don't think there'll be much left,' I say, gazing at the ancient packet of green lentils. I pick it up. It says: 'Best Before 2006.'

'Oh, you don't want to worry about those,' says Dad. 'Best Befores are a guideline. They have to put those on for the law, but food can be fine for years after that date.'

'Even so, Dad. This is out of date by a long time. I think we should throw it away.'

'All right. Probably best. What else have we got?'

After I have discarded all the packets and jars that are out of date by two years or more (Dad insists on keeping the others), along with the mouse-nibbled packet of Rice Krispies, we are left with a small pile of sorry-looking items.

'Hmm,' says Dad, his face falling as he looks at them. 'Not sure what I can make with these. But I'll give it a go.'

He grabs a pan and the bag of potatoes and begins to hum – something I haven't heard him do for a long time. The atmosphere lifts, and I find a candle in a drawer and stick it on a chipped saucer and light it, just like I've read in books. Now it feels like we're in wartime, struggling to cope with rationing and air raids. It's a game, like 'let's pretend', and I like made-up games.

'Dad,' I say, remembering something, 'have you heard of a girl who wrote a diary in the war and then died? And her father got the diary published a couple of years later?'

'Anne Frank,' says Dad, filling the kettle with water and searching for the potato peeler. 'She and her family hid in an annexe in an office building in Amsterdam during the war. They lived there for two years.'

'They couldn't go out?' I ask.

'No. Jews weren't allowed to walk the streets, buy anything or be in public places. They were arrested if they did.'

I nod. 'So she was real?'

'Oh yes. She wrote a diary all the time she was in hiding. And then the family was betrayed and they were sent to a concentration camp. Anne died there.'

'Oh.' I recall Mae wiping her eyes as she told me about the book. I can see why now. It is very sad, just like the one I read about the German boy. 'Did Anne like reading?' I ask.

'Yes, she was very keen on reading. And learning. She wanted to be a journalist.'

I nod. Anne was my sort of person, by the sound of it. I must definitely read her book next.

Dad says, 'Ta-dah!' and serves up dinner. My plate is heaped with something that looks lumpy and yellow with pink bits mixed in.

'What is it?' I ask cautiously.

'Potato surprise!' he says, beaming.

I smile back. It's nice to see him so happy. And the food, once I start eating, isn't all that bad really. There are some squidgy bits and some crunchy bits, but there's cheese and potato and some tomatoes, I think. And it's hot and filling and I eat it all. 'Thanks, Dad. I like it a lot.'

'You like it *very much*,' he corrects me.

'Is there any more?'

He laughs. 'Sorry. The cupboards are bare. And I *will* go to the shop tomorrow.'

I give him a look.

'I will! I will – I finished the proofread of the

journal today, so I can go first thing in the morning. You can help me make a list, so I don't forget anything.' He gives me a look of barely suppressed excitement. 'And . . . I wasn't going to tell you, but . . . I'm preparing my manuscript to send out to publishers!'

'Your History?' I say, amazed. 'It's finished?'

He nods. 'It is. It needs polishing, and of course there are always new scientific discoveries that will impact on lemon growing, but I feel now is the time.'

'Oh, Dad!' Impulsively, I get up and hug him.

He flinches slightly, then gives me a couple of light pats on the back, as though not quite sure what to do with his arms.

'That's brilliant, well done you!'

Carefully, he pushes me away from him again. 'I am very pleased with it,' he says. I almost don't recognise him, he's smiling so much. His face looks completely different. If you'd shown me a photograph of him at this moment, I'd have asked, 'Who's that?' I think maybe he used to smile more, before Mum died, but it's so difficult to remember.

5

The next day, I'm in an art lesson with Mae when I say, 'My dad's written a book and it's going to be published.' Then I take a sharp breath in. My own words have surprised me. Why did I tell her?

Mae's paintbrush, halfway between paint pot and paper, stops in mid-air. She looks very impressed. 'Really? What kind of book?'

'It's an important historical one,' I say. I blush slightly. 'It's called *A History of the Lemon.*'

'The lemon?' asks Mae, looking puzzled. 'Which lemon?'

'*The* lemon,' I say. 'I mean, *all* lemons. It's about lemons through history: where they came from, what they've been used for, all that.'

'Wow. It sounds big.' She puts the paintbrush back into the pot.

'It is. He's been working on it for years.'

Mae nods. 'That would be really amazing, to have your name on the front cover of a book.'

'I know.'

'I want to write books when I'm older,' Mae says.

I blurt out, 'Me too!'

I've never told anyone that before. We stare at each other, bound by this invisible ambition.

Mae looks very serious now. There is something in her eyes. Recognition. 'I knew you were a kindred spirit,' she whispers.

I take a breath and let it out very slowly. 'You've read *Anne of Green Gables*.'

'Of course I have. We're like Anne and Diana.'

'I want to be Anne,' I say quickly.

'I think you are,' she agrees. 'Because you have red hair and you read a lot. And I have dark hair and cry at everything, like Diana.' She grins suddenly, and it's like the sun has come out.

We have become friends and I didn't even mean to.

6

It becomes unspoken that we sit together. We go into the playground together at break. We take our books and go to sit in a quiet place. If it's raining, we go to the school library. Mr Simmons has known me a long time and even though we're not supposed to be in the library at lunchtime, he's been letting me in since Year Three. Now he smiles at me when I come in with Mae, and nods, as though he knows something we don't.

Mae lends me her copy of Anne Frank's diary. It is gripping. I barely eat or drink for the time it takes me to read it. I would skip the lessons at school if I dared. When I finish it, I almost cry. There is a hot, tickly feeling at the back of my throat, but I swallow it down. Anne had inner strength – a lot of it. There's no use me crying over her story when she's been dead for years. Instead, I should be learning to be more like her.

Anne had ambitions and dreams – lots of them. She wanted to be a writer, so she started her diary as practice. There was so much she wanted to do with her life – and she didn't get the chance.

What if I die before I can become a writer?

Mae and I discuss this seriously.

'We should start writing now,' she says. 'So that we have a legacy to leave if we die young. Like Anne.'

'Actually,' I say cautiously, 'I have already written some stories.'

Mae's eyes light up. 'That's cool! Can I read them?'

The next day, I bring one in to show her. It's about a girl and her friends who survive a huge nuclear war. They have to rebuild society and make new laws and find out how to kill and eat their food and everything. It's fifty-three pages of my notebook. My hands feel slippery when I give it to Mae. What if she doesn't like it? Could we still be friends?

She reads it over lunch break, her eyes never

leaving the words, turning the pages steadily and in silence. I watch her as she reads, trying to work out what she thinks, feeling my heart skip every time she smiles or her eyes open wide in surprise at something in the story. And then I try to look away, because I hate people watching me while I read – but I can't help glancing back all the time, to see if she's nearing the end.

Eventually, she closes the book and sighs. Then she gives me the biggest smile, and relief floods through me.

'I love it,' she says. 'It's so exciting. And the scene where they have to kill the rabbit gave me the shivers! The ending is perfect, but I want to know what happens next. Are you going to write a sequel?'

I hesitate. 'I was going to. But then I had an idea for a different story, so I started writing that instead.'

'Well, I think there should be a sequel to this one,' she says. And then she adds impulsively, 'We could write it together! I've got loads of ideas of what they could do next!' She stops. 'Unless . . . I mean, it's your story . . . you might not want me to join in.'

I've never written a story with someone else before. But if I were to choose a writing partner, it would be Mae. Of course it would. I smile back at her, and that's that settled.

Mae brings in a brand-new A4 hardback note-book, and over the coming weeks we sit together every lunchtime and write another chapter. I do the writing because my handwriting is neater. Mae sits with her eyes closed and thinks out loud.

'When she meets the stranger,' she says, 'she should be really nervous and frightened because he reminds her of someone bad from her past.'

I smile. It's good, and it sparks off a new idea in me. We work well together, contributing ideas and discussing plot points. I borrow a book called *How to Write* from the public library and we devour it.

'We could get this story published,' Mae says.

'No,' I say. 'We need to write for years and years before we're good enough.'

But Mae is impatient. The next day, she comes into school brimming with enthusiasm. 'We could put it online! People would pay to read it – we could make some money!'

I am tempted. Money would be very helpful. There never seems to be much of it at home, and there are things I would like to buy.

'I don't know how to do that,' I say.

'I do,' Mae tells me confidently. 'I looked at a forum last night on the computer.'

I think of Dad's computer in his library, hardly ever switched on. I wish I could use it, but it's on his desk, and he's always there. If I had money, I could have a computer of my own.

'Let's do it,' I say.

7

'Can I go round to Mae's tomorrow after school?' I say to Dad.

He frowns at his manuscript. 'Who's Mae?'

'The new girl. Well, not new any more.'

'Why do you want to go to her house?' He licks his finger and turns a few pages, his eyes scanning the lines of text. 'Ah – there's the reference.'

I'm not quite sure how to say the words. 'She's my best friend.'

He looks up at this. 'Best friend? You have a best friend?'

It's almost like he's saying, 'You have a unicorn?' – he sounds *that* surprised.

'Yes. She likes books. We're writing a story together.'

He stares at me for a moment as though he can't quite understand. Then he smiles. 'Well, that's nice.'

I hadn't realised I've been holding my breath. 'So I can go?'

He nods. 'Why not?'

I am euphoric.

8

Mae's house is semi-detached, separated from the road by a small front garden. There's a tidy flower bed with pink and red flowers in it, and paving slabs leading to the front door. I have to take my shoes off when I go in, which seems strange to me. If I took my shoes off at home, my feet would freeze. But here there are soft carpets and no draughts.

We've come in Mae's mum's car, which is shiny and clean and doesn't make any weird noises when you drive it. I sit between Mae and her brother Christopher, who is eight and picks his nose but is otherwise okay – I mean 'all right'. Mae's mum asks us about our day and smiles at me in the rear-view mirror. She is middle-sized, with a soft, round face and untidy hair and she smiles a lot. She's so warm and friendly in a 'mum' sort of way that it gives me a kind of pain deep inside. I make an effort to smile back at her.

Mae says to her mum, 'We're going up to my room,' as soon as we get in the door, so I follow her upstairs.

Mae's room is a hotchpotch of things. There's one wall of beautiful patterned wallpaper, which appears to be stuck on with sticky tape along one side. On another wall, Mae has drawn large black rectangles onto the white background. One of the rectangles is full of felt-tip patterns in blues and greens. Another rectangle is only partially completed. There's a wardrobe and a chest of drawers and a bed, with a pale green bedspread covered in daisies. A big green oval rug on the floor takes up most of the space and has tiny white daisies on it. The room feels like an art gallery in a forest.

And there are books, of course. *Lots* of books, stacked two deep on a bookshelf and spilling out in paper waterfalls onto the floor. Just seeing them makes me feel instantly at home.

'Oh, *Wonder*!' I cry, pulling it out. 'I haven't read it!'

'You can borrow it.' Mae reaches into a bedside drawer and produces a laptop. It's sleek and shiny and silver, and I marvel. I didn't realise she had her own laptop; I thought there was a family computer. How many people would have to buy our story in order for me to afford one of those?

'Borrow anything you like.' Mae nods at me while she waits for her computer to start.

I crawl along beside the bookshelf, staring hard to make sure I don't miss anything. There are books here by Jacqueline Wilson, Louise Rennison, Celia Rees, Hilary McKay and Linda Newbery. There are stories about mermaids, girls with magical powers and boys getting into trouble. I pluck out *Holes*, *The Tail of Emily Windsnap*, *Liar & Spy* and *Pea's Book of Holidays*. Mae's taste in books is so similar to mine it gives me a rush of warmth. I had thought I was the only one whose life was consumed by stories. The only one who preferred imaginary worlds to the real one.

Stuffed in the wrong way round is a book by Susan Cooper. 'This is one of the Dark Is Rising books,' I say. 'It's one of my favourite series.'

'I liked it,' Mae agrees, 'but I didn't cry at it.'

I smile to myself. To get a ten out of ten from Mae, the book must leave her in floods of tears.

'Here we are.' Mae pats the bed next to her. 'Come and look at this.'

For the next hour we pore over the internet, reading all kinds of advice about how to publish your book online.

'See? If we made it into an ebook, we could sell it properly through a store,' Mae says. 'I have a bank account. Or we could set up a new one.'

There's lots of help out there, though after a while all the information makes my head spin, so Mae suggests going downstairs for some fresh air.

Mae's mum is in the dining room. There's a mass of silky fabric spread across the table, and she's picking silver pins out of a pot and carefully pinning it together.

'This is beautiful,' I say, staring. The fabric is pale green, with a sheen so it looks gold from some angles, and tiny purple embroidered flowers. 'What are you making?'

'A new skirt.' Mae's mum straightens up and rubs her back. 'It's pretty, isn't it?'

'Gorgeous.' I want to touch it but don't dare. I haven't washed my hands. Instead, I stare and stare at the green-gold waves. It reminds me of a painting my mother did that now hangs in the hallway where you can't really see it in the gloom. She painted a field at sunset, with wild flowers and the green of the grass turning to gold in the sun's rays. A lump comes to my throat and I swallow it down quickly.

Luckily, Mae hasn't noticed. 'Come on,' she says. 'Let's go outside.'

I follow her, casting a longing look back at the dining table. 'Does your mum make a lot of clothes?' I hesitate after I say 'a lot' because Dad doesn't like the phrase. But Mae doesn't correct me.

'I guess so,' says Mae. 'She used to make loads for me and Christopher, but not so much now.'

'Why not?' I'd expire with happiness if I had a skirt made out of that amazing material.

Mae shrugs. 'It's kind of embarrassing when your mum makes your clothes. I'd rather have something from a shop, wouldn't you?'

No, I think, but I don't say it. Things from shops are all the same. I like the idea of making and owning something unique, something that no one else in the world will have. Like a story that no one else could write, or a painting that no one else could paint.

Christopher is out in the garden with a magnifying glass and a big plastic tub. His fingers are muddy.

'What are you doing?' asks Mae.

'Making a worm farm,' he says, without looking up.

'A what?'

'A wormery,' I say, watching him scrabble around in the dirt. 'Dad proofread a book about sustainability once. It had all kinds of ideas in it for growing your own food, making your own butter and that kind of thing. A wormery is like a compost bin, only with worms, so the stuff breaks down faster – more quickly.'

Mae screws up her little nose. 'Eurgh. You're not bringing it in the house, are you? Mum'll go mad.'

'Of course not.' Christopher reaches into the flower bed and pulls out a worm by one end.

'You shouldn't touch them with your bare hands,' I tell him. 'Our skin is too acid – you'll hurt it.'

'Oh, that's rubbish,' says Christopher, putting the worm into his tub. 'Besides, I'm not touching it for long.'

'It's not rubbish, it's true,' I say. 'And I don't think that's the right kind of worm anyway.'

He turns to stare at me. 'What are you talking about?'

I feel a bit nervous because Dad worked on the

book a long time ago – at least six months – and I can't remember it very well. 'I think you have to get special worms. From a shop.'

Christopher turns away again with a snort. 'I'm sure these'll be fine. All worms do the same thing, after all. Stuff goes in one end, and soil comes out the other.'

He's wrong, but I don't feel confident enough to argue with him. Mae told me once that Christopher only likes books about facts, so now I'm not quite sure what to say to him. How do you talk to someone who doesn't like stories?

'Yuck,' says Mae, looking away. 'Come on, Calypso, let's do something else. This is disgusting.'

Their garden has an apple tree in the middle with a rope swing. I have a go but I keep falling off – and then I spot something hidden down the end of the garden, half buried in shrubs.

'Is that a Wendy house?' I say with a gasp.

'Oh – yeah,' says Mae. 'It's kind of overgrown, though. You can't really use it.'

'You don't use it?' I can't believe it. She has a *real* Wendy house! When I was younger, I read a story about a girl and her friends who had a secret meeting house in the woods: a dilapidated, falling-down sort of place of their own. And there was another story about a boy who lived in a treehouse and ate berries and roots and had a pet squirrel. I tried to persuade Dad to build me a treehouse, but he said he didn't know how. For months I dreamed that I had my own miniature den in the garden – and Mae actually has one that she doesn't use!

I run over and push open the little door. It's square inside and quite big – bigger than you'd think from the outside – and the shrubs have grown up to cover the windows, so it's very dark. But there's room for me to get in and sit on the floor, and there'd be room for three or four other children our age too.

'Don't sit down,' says Mae. 'I think it's damp.'

It's too late, and my school skirt is going to need a wash and a dry. Something I'll have to remember to do when I get home.

'Oh,' I say in some disappointment. 'You need a rug in here.'

'That'd get damp too,' says Mae. 'There's damp coming up from underneath.'

'Can't we fix it?' I say. 'This would be such a great place to do our writing!' Images are bursting into my head like fireworks: cushions; curtains; lamps;

notebooks; me and Mae sitting together with pens and pencils, plotting and planning and writing for hours and hours.

'It's too dark,' says Mae. 'But we could cut down some of the plants, maybe? Then the light would get in.'

'Why haven't you done it before?' I say, enthusiasm bubbling out of me. 'It'd be the first thing I'd do if I moved to a new place and found a real Wendy house in the garden!'

Mae shrugs. 'Well, Christopher wasn't interested and I didn't want to play in it on my own.'

I give a little sigh. I've always played on my own. There's never been a sibling to play with. After me, Mum and Dad decided not to have any more children. Mum used to say something about us being a 'perfect family triangle', though now I wonder if she said it in a happy or a sad way. I can't remember her voice any more – if I had a brother or a sister, I could talk to them about it . . . I tried to ask Dad once why I was an only child, but he shrugged and said that was just the way things were. But now I have Mae. And she is almost as good as a sister.

'I'll do it up with you,' I say. 'Give it a makeover.'

Mae smiles. 'I like that idea. Mum could make

some curtains. And maybe Dad can find out how to make the floor waterproof.'

'I'd swap my library for a Wendy house,' I say, looking around at the bare walls and feeling a rush of excitement. Visions dance before my eyes: flickering candlelight, shelves of books in every size and colour, strings of beads hanging at the windows . . . It would be the most perfect place in the world: a retreat, a secret just for me and whoever I chose to invite.

'You have a *library*?' asks Mae, her eyes widening.

'We have two,' I say proudly. 'Dad has one and I have my own. In the spare room.' The room that used to be Mum's studio. For a split-second, I think of Mae's mum – her smiling, warm face – and I feel a sudden pang. Of pain? Or jealousy?

I would swap my library – *and* a Wendy house – to have my mum back.

Mae's mouth has fallen open. 'You have a whole *room* for your books? Can I see?' she says reverently. 'Can I come round one day?'

'Oh. Well . . .' I've never invited anyone to my house before. I've never really wanted to. What would Dad say? For a moment I don't know how to answer. Then something in me strengthens. I have a best friend! It doesn't mean I *don't* have inner strength. Best friends are good! 'Of course,' I say confidently. 'Any time you like.'

'Mae! Calypso!' Mae's mum is calling from the back door. I crawl out of the little house and we head back across the grass. 'I should be taking you home soon, Calypso, shouldn't I?'

'Oh, Mum, can't Calypso stay for supper?' asks Mae.

I feel almost light-headed at the idea and my stomach growls in response. I bet they don't have beans on toast for dinner.

Her mum looks at me. 'I don't know. Is that all right with your dad, Calypso? Didn't we agree I'd bring you back at five?'

But at home, I'll have to make my own dinner, and just this once it would be so nice . . .

'Oh, I'm sure he won't mind,' I say airily. 'He's working.'

Mae's mum says, 'I'm happy for you to stay for supper if you think it'll be all right. I should give your dad a ring, though, just so he knows.'

Dad hates to be interrupted while he's working. And what if he said no? What if he said I had to come home at five, like we arranged?

A sense of rebellion grips me. 'No, it's okay,' I say, using the word deliberately and relishing it. 'He'll be busy. I don't usually see him until after supper time.'

She gives me a strange look, but before she can ask me anything else, Christopher, walking towards us, trips over his shoelace and drops the tub of worms all over the grass and his mum's feet.

Mae's mum shrieks, '*Christopher!*' and I feel an unbidden bubble of laughter build up inside me. Thank goodness for worm distractions! I hold back the giggle: Mae's mum is cross, and she might be cross with me too if I laugh at her. And then she might take me home.

'Oh no!' Christopher says, scrabbling around, trying to pick them all up.

I press my lips together at the funny sight.

'Help me, Mae,' he begs.

'No way!' says Mae, looking horrified. 'Come on, Calypso, let's go to my room and draw plans for the Wendy house.'

She pulls me away, and as we run I glance back once more to see Christopher dumping handfuls of worms into his bucket while his mum scolds him and shakes worms off her shoes. I feel grateful to Christopher for diverting attention away from me. And the situation with the worms really is very funny. It's like a cartoon, and I wish I could capture the silliness of the moment. I like laughing. If I had a brother, would I laugh more at home?

9

Mae and I have a lovely half an hour drawing diagrams and making plans for the renovation of the Wendy house. I completely lose track of time, just like when I'm reading. But this isn't something I'm doing alone, in my own head. I'm beginning to see why so many people have a best friend. Mae's ideas make me smile because they're brilliant and I know I wouldn't have thought of them myself. Lots of her suggestions spark my own ideas, and together we develop them. It feels great. It's twice as much fun to create something when you do it with someone else. I want the afternoon to go on for ever.

Supper is beef stroganoff. I've never had it before. It's creamy and warming and tastes so delicious I wonder if there can be anything better in the world.

Mae's mum smiles. 'You were hungry.'

'Yes,' I say, looking at my plate. There isn't a single

grain of rice left. I know there's more on the stove – I've seen it – but Mae's mum doesn't offer any more and it would be rude to ask. Instead, though, she does bring out a big chocolate mousse. Pudding!

'We never have pudding in my house,' I say enthusiastically, putting a spoonful into my mouth. The taste is heavenly.

'I love pudding,' says Mae. 'Treacle tart, yum. Apple pie. Ice cream.'

I can't remember the last time I had any of those things at home.

'Crumble,' says Christopher with his mouth full. His nails are still brown with dirt, even though his mum has made him wash them three times. She made him put the worms back in the flower beds too, and he spent the first half of the meal complaining about the unfairness. It made me want to giggle again.

'What do you usually have for supper, Calypso?' she asks, and her voice sounds light and friendly.

'Oh, all kinds of things,' I assure her. Being here, in this nice warm house, with this wonderful food, makes me feel ashamed of my own. I can't tell her I cook my own supper and that it's usually beans on toast.

'Does your mum like cooking?' she asks.

I dig my spoon into the bottom of the bowl. 'My mum died,' I say without looking up.

Mae gasps. 'What? I didn't know that!'

There is a pause. I keep scraping the bottom of my bowl so that I don't have to look up. I imagine them all exchanging frantic glances: what do we say next?

'I'm so sorry,' Mae's mum says, after a moment. 'Was it recent?'

'No. Years ago, when I was five.'

There isn't any mousse left in the bowl, but I keep scraping for the tiny bits to avoid looking up.

'I didn't know,' Mae says in an agonised whisper, and I get the impression she isn't saying it to me but to her mum.

I don't know what to say. What else is there? My vision seems to have narrowed to the white china bowl in my hands. Everything around it is in shadow.

And then Christopher does a huge burp and the shadows disappear.

'What?' he says defensively.

'That's revolting,' his mum says sharply.

Christopher tries to protest. 'It just came out of nowhere.'

'No, it didn't. You always know when it's coming, and the polite thing to do is to close your mouth and apologise afterwards.'

'I *didn't* know it was coming!'

I was relieved at first when everyone was distracted from me, but now I feel anxious. I wish Christopher would just apologise and keep quiet, not argue back. I can see him getting crosser, and his mum's voice is getting higher.

'It's just a question of manners, Christopher, and you're turning into a savage.'

'I am *not*!'

'Don't talk back to me!'

I clench my hands into fists under the table and feel chilly waves pass over me. Their voices are harsh, like they hate each other.

'Shall I take the bowls out?' says Mae in an 'I'm bored by this' voice. She gets up and starts to clear.

'I'll help.' I almost knock over the water jug in my haste.

The argument subsides, to my great relief, and Christopher slinks off sulkily.

When everything's cleared away and I've made sure to say how nice all the food was, Mae's mum says it's time to take me home.

'Christopher!' she calls. 'Can you come and get in the car? It's time to take Calypso home.'

To my utter astonishment, Christopher appears looking perfectly cheerful again, holding some kind of puzzle toy.

'I solved it,' he tells us, putting on his trainers. 'It's supposed to take half an hour and I did it in ten minutes. That makes me a genius.'

His mum laughs. 'You wish!'

I am baffled. How can their argument be over so quickly? Why aren't they still cross with each other? All that emotion, all those angry words – where did they go? I feel quite weak as I sink into the car seat, and I barely hear a word anyone says on the short journey through the fading light. Dad and I never argue. If I get cross with Dad, he never argues back. He just retreats into silence and I go to my room feeling like a cloud, thundery and dark. Sometimes it takes hours for me to feel normal again. I could never switch from anger to cheerfulness in the space of a few short minutes.

'Is this the right place, Calypso?' asks Mae's mum.

I look through the window at our house. Set back from the road, detached, surrounded by overgrown trees and shrubs, with a small iron gate that has sunk on its hinges so it no longer shuts properly. Our house looks dark, unloved and unhappy, in sharp contrast to the warm and cosy house I've just left. For the first time ever, I feel reluctant to come home.

'This is your house?' Mae is leaning out of the window. 'It looks like the house from *The Amazing Mr Blunden*.'

'What's that?'

'It's a really old ghost story. Ooh, do you have any ghosts?'

'No,' I say sharply, undoing my seat belt. 'No, we don't.'

Her face falls. 'Shame.'

'I'll come up to the house with you,' Mae's mum says, turning off the engine and undoing her seat belt.

'No – no, you don't need to.'

I'm out of the car as quick as a flash and standing on the pavement with my bag. I don't want her to see inside. What would she think of our cold, untidy house with its dusty corners and peeling paint?

I lean in through the open door. 'Honestly. I've got my own key.' I hold it up to prove it.

'I just think it'd be nice if I said hello to your dad,' she says, and her door clunk-clicks open. She puts one foot on the ground. 'We've only spoken on the phone briefly – it seems rude that we haven't yet met when you and Mae are such good friends.'

'Look.' I point to the window to the left of our front door. A light is on, twinkling through the branches of the dark tree. 'That's Dad's library. The light means he's working, and he hates to be disturbed.'

Mae shouts from the back of the car, 'He's going to be published!'

Mae's mum hesitates.

I smile at her reassuringly. 'He'll be all grumpy if we disturb him in the middle of writing, honestly.'

She glances at the library window and then makes up her mind. 'All right, if you're sure. I'll watch you go in, though.'

'Bye, Calypso!' Mae calls, waving.

Christopher is picking his nose again, trying to pretend he isn't by turning his head to one side.

I walk up the garden path, put my key in the door and turn it, pushing down on the handle at the same time. I step inside the house, turn to wave at the car, see Mae's mum get back in and drive away. Then I close the door and stand in the gloomy hallway on the cold stone flagging, listening to the silence and feeling the draught swirl around my ankles.

10

I am halfway up the stairs when Dad comes out of his library.

'Calypso!' he says, sounding surprised. 'I thought I heard the door. Have you had a good time?'

'Yes,' I say, 'thank you.' *Good* doesn't even come close.

He smiles. 'I'm glad. Shall we have some food?'

'I . . . er . . . I ate at Mae's.'

He ducks back into the library, and reappears, his eyebrows pulled right together in the middle. 'It's nearly seven o'clock! That's not what we agreed!'

I knew it! I just *knew* he wouldn't have noticed the time. Mae's mum would have noticed. Mae's mum would have been *worried*. But Dad has been too absorbed in his work, as always.

'I thought it would be *okay*,' I say, deliberately

using the word to aggravate him. 'You were working anyway.'

'You're *two hours* late! That's not acceptable, Calypso. I'm surprised that Mae's mother didn't contact me. Very irresponsible attitude to a child's safety.'

I can't bear him to have a go at one of the nicest people I've ever met.

'She wanted to,' I say crossly, 'but I didn't want her to disturb you.' And I was afraid you'd say no. I cross my fingers behind my back. 'I was thinking of *you*, Dad. You knew where I was. You *know* I'm sensible.'

'That's not the point.' My father is using his 'authoritative' voice. 'You may be sensible but you are only ten years old and you are a Vulnerable Person.'

I am suddenly exhausted. 'Whatever.' I know he hates this expression too, and I see his jaw clench. But I turn away. 'I'm going to bed.'

As I trudge up the rest of the uncarpeted, smudged and dusty stairs, I wonder briefly what Dad is going to have for supper. Then I feel angry with myself for even having the thought. He's a grown-up, he can sort it himself.

I get into bed with *Over Sea, Under Stone*, one of the books I've borrowed from Mae. I must lend her something in return. I have loads of books I know she'll love. I must have another look through the shelves in Dad's library too, because there are lots of Mum's books there, waiting for me to be old enough to read them. Murder mysteries and historical stories about highwaymen and beautiful women, and ghost stories that might have frightened me when I was younger. I haven't looked at the shelves for a couple of years, so I might be old enough for them now.

I am soon engrossed in the book, and my room is swept away by the sounds of gulls crying, the metallic slap of sail ropes against masts and ancient magic. I borrowed it from the town library once before, but that was ages ago. I keep reading and reading, mainly because deep in the recesses of my mind I know that when I stop reading I will remember the lovely afternoon I had at Mae's house, where there was laughter and beautiful fabric and a Wendy house and a worm disaster. And it will make me sad, and I don't want to feel sad.

So I keep reading and reading until my eyes close halfway through a sentence, and I fall asleep with my head creasing the pages.

11

The next Saturday I stand in front of Mum's hallway painting for a long time: the one of the field in the sunset. Even though I've switched on the overhead light, the colours don't sing in the way I remember. In the end, I climb on a chair and take the picture down. It's big and heavy.

'What are you doing?' calls Dad from the library. He's in there again, working away on his History. He works most weekends, so I've got used to occupying myself. I wonder what Mae's doing today. Going swimming, maybe, or to the park. I can't do that, but I can escape in other ways.

'Just borrowing a picture,' I call back.

I lug the picture up the stairs and into Dad's bedroom at the front of the house. The sun is out today and its rays are sliding and dancing through the top of the apple tree that blocks the library window below. I prop the picture up against the end of the bed and step back to look at it.

Yes. That's better. It IS as beautiful as that shiny fabric. Green and gold and hazy and beautiful, with tiny white, red and blue wild flowers. I sit on the floor and gaze at it for a long time. I can imagine how Mum must have felt when she painted this. Dad's bedroom, with its worn carpet and faded bedsheets, dissolves and now I can hear the sound of birdsong and the wind in the grass. The sun warms my head and I know that if I reach out one hand, I'll be able to touch the waving heads of the poppies. In the far distance, just out of sight, a gypsy caravan pulled by a carthorse slowly makes its way down a grassy lane. And three children are building a den in the middle of a nearby copse, scratching their legs on brambles and getting muddy splashes from the stream.

I stay in that grassy, sunny world for as long as I can. Mum is there too, I'm sure, somewhere just behind me. If I turn round she'll vanish, but right now I know she's there. I can almost remember her face from my own memory and not from her photograph. I think she's laughing.

12

As the days go by I spend more and more time at Mae's house. It becomes easy to say to Dad in the morning, 'I'm going round to Mae's after school, all right?'

To begin with, he looks slightly puzzled, as though he can't quite work out why I want to be with her so much. And then he looks pleased, and gives a firm nod, saying, 'Good. It's nice that you have a friend.' But sometimes he looks pained, and I can't quite work out why. He doesn't miss me when I'm not there, I know that. He's told me so many times that he's an independent person and doesn't need others around him to be happy. So I'm not really sure why my being out would bother him. And to be honest, I don't let it worry me because I enjoy going to Mae's so much.

Mae and I are keen to start work on the Wendy

house and turn it into our secret writing hideaway.

Her dad tries to persuade us it's not worth saving. 'It's only fit for firewood,' he says. 'I've been meaning to chop it up since we got here.'

Mae's lip wobbles. 'No, no!' she cries. 'You can't – we're going to make it good again.'

Her dad frowns. He's not a big man, but he's kind of wide, with very broad shoulders and very short hair. He's nice but not warm in the way that Mae's mum is. I feel a bit nervous around him, especially when he frowns.

'Maybe you can have a new one for next summer,' he says. 'Honestly, Mae, it's rotting through.'

'No, it isn't.' Mae stamps her foot. 'It's going to be our special place! It's *fine*.'

'It isn't! Look!' He reaches out to the corner of the roof and breaks off a piece, crumbling it in his hand.

Mae gives an outraged gasp. 'Don't do that! Leave it alone! If you're not going to help us, we'll do it ourselves!'

I feel that cold wave of nausea that I get when people argue. They argue quite often in Mae's house, and although it never seems to last long, I always get anxious. And sometimes, like now, Mae can be quite rude to her father, and I can't quite believe she speaks to him that way. I wouldn't want to argue with him.

But he gives a resigned shrug and says, 'If you insist. I'll help if it'll keep you quiet.'

Mae beams at him. 'Thanks, Dad.' And just like that, it's over, and she's got her way, and I can't decide if I'm appalled or impressed.

After a lot of puffing and panting, he manages to raise the whole thing off the ground and put it on bricks, so the floor can start to dry out. Mae and I cut down the plants and shrubs that have grown up all around it, so that light can get in through the windows.

Her dad's right. It's not in very good condition. The roof part has a thick felt layer that's rotted away, and there are some nasty nail spikes sticking out of one corner. But Mae and I are fired with enthusiasm at the opportunity to build something together, something just for us, and so our diagrams and plans grow by the day, along with our ambitions.

Mae's mum finishes the skirt she's been making and puts it on for me one day. It's so beautiful I want to cry.

She sees my expression. 'I have some fabric left over,' she says gently. 'Would you like me to make you something? It's not enough for something to wear, I'm afraid, but I could make you a bag.'

I swallow and nod. And then I have to hide in the toilet for a few moments to get control of myself. I don't want her to see me cry. I want her to think I have inner strength. I'm not sure Mae understands about inner strength, though. She cries in front of me quite a lot. Like the day we find a dead pigeon in the garden that's obviously lost a fight with a cat.

'I hate cats!' she sobs. 'That poor bird!'

I put my arms around her and she grabs me back, wetting my shoulder with her tears. Her body heaves and shakes as she cries and cries, and I hold her close. Something inside me is tight and sore, like I'm feeling what she feels, like I want to cry too. But I don't. Instead, I stay strong for her.

Mae's mum cuddles her too when she finds out about the pigeon. She hugs Mae and Christopher quite a lot, I've noticed. Sometimes they say they don't want her to, but she does it anyway and then they smile. I feel envious. I miss hugs so much, and seeing Mae's mum hug them makes me happy-sad all at once. I try to hug Mae every day when I see her, because I know it makes me feel good.

Dressing up makes me feel good too. On the Monday of the half-term break, Mae's mum offers to make some curtains for the writing den and produces a huge bag of fabric for us to choose from.

'This is amazing!' I sigh, running my fingers over a thick satin brocade. 'Far too beautiful for our den. It should be made into a ballgown or something.'

'Wrap it round your waist,' suggests Mae. 'Like a big skirt.'

'Oh, I couldn't. What if I spoil it?'

Mae's mum comes in with another bag of fabric. 'This is more cotton stuff,' she says.

'Mum, can we dress up in this?' asks Mae.

Her mum hesitates. 'I suppose so, as long as you're careful. Don't take it outside. And wash your hands so that you don't get any of it dirty.'

Mae and I have a BRILLIANT time. There are soft silky pieces, some velvet, more satin, summery flowery cottons and some very thin material like the stuff wedding veils are made out of.

I swathe myself in a kaleidoscope of rainbows and imagine I am a princess of a faraway kingdom.

'We should do the poem *The Lady of Shalott*,' says Mae, 'like they do in *Anne of Green Gables*.'

'Only without the boat,' I say. 'Anne ended up in the river. Your mum would kill us if we damaged her material.'

'We can make a pretend boat in here, though,' Mae says, waving a silver-draped arm at the sitting room. 'We could build it out of chairs. Do you know the poem?'

'Some of it.'

She stares at me. 'Can I do something with your hair?'

I touch my tight red curls. 'Do what with it?'

She fetches a brush. 'Sit down.'

Brushing my hair does not improve its appearance. It simply makes the springy coils stand out from my head in a carroty cloud.

'It's amazing,' says Mae, getting the brush stuck more than once. 'Like in old books where the girls had to sleep with their hair in rags to get ringlets. Yours just does it by itself. I wish mine did that.'

'No, you don't,' I say. 'You have the most beautiful hair ever.' And it's true. Mae's hair is thick and black and straight and glossy like treacle. Her brother has the same black hair and so does her mum – an ebony waterfall that hangs right down to her waist. I think her mum is Chinese, or maybe Japanese. I'd like to know but I worry that it would be rude to ask.

Mae teases my carroty cloud of hair and smoothes some kind of perfumed cream through my wiry curls. I gasp when I look in the mirror above the fireplace. Suddenly I look like a completely different person – more grown up, sophisticated.

'That's – that's . . .' I stroke my hair, which smells delicious, like a very expensive dessert. I don't think anyone has ever done my hair before. The person in the mirror looks like someone I would like to know. And in a tiny way – just for a flash, a minuscule moment – she looks like my mother. I stare at myself, noting the big eyes with the gingery eyelashes, the sprinkling of freckles over my nose and cheeks, the slightly pink mouth that lifts up at one corner, just like my mother's in the photograph I have of her in my room. She is staring back at me from the mirror, through time, and I can't look away.

'Wow,' says Mae's mum, breaking into my thoughts. 'You look like you've just stepped out of one of those romantic paintings.'

I blush and turn away from the mirror. I know the ones she means: Guinevere, with long flowing hair and medieval robes. Titania, queen of the fairies. Maybe in time my frizzy ginger mop will turn into the beautiful auburn tresses of my mother – just as Anne's did in the stories.

'It's perfect for *The Lady of Shalott*,' says Mae.

We drag a couple of chairs into the middle of the floor, which is tricky because we're both draped in large pieces of fabric, and push them seats-together to make a boat.

In the poem, the Lady of Shalott has been imprisoned in a tower under a curse. She can't look out of the window, only into a mirror, and she spends all her days weaving and dreaming of being rescued. Then one day the dashing Sir Lancelot comes riding by and she can't resist rushing to the window to see him properly – and the mirror cracks, the Lady runs down the tower stairs to get into a boat and drifts downstream towards Camelot. But by the time she gets there, she's dead, and Lancelot sees her beautiful dead body and wonders who she was. And that's the end of the poem.

It's very romantic. I don't really understand how she dies, but I suppose if you're under an evil curse then there's not much you can do about it.

Once the scene is set, I do the bit of the poem

where the Lady is weaving in her tower room and runs to the window to look out at the handsome Sir Lancelot riding by. Then I stagger dramatically, struck by the curse, and clamber into the boat. Mae has to help me with this bit because I get my own foot stuck in my skirt and the knot at my waist comes undone in a not-very-romantic way. But in the end, I'm safely in the cushiony boat, and I lie down on my back with my hands crossed over my chest and stare up at the ceiling.

'You're supposed to have flowers,' says Mae. She looks around. 'Here.' She thrusts a piece of white cotton at me. It's printed with blue poppies.

'Is that the best we've got?' I say, screwing up my nose. 'Haven't you got any real flowers?'

'Hang on.' Mae brightens. 'I've got an idea. Back in a minute.' She disappears out of the big French doors, and I practise lying still in the boat and imagine the gentle river lapping at the wooden sides. My eyelids start to droop.

'Here you are!'

I jolt awake as Mae hands me a handful of bright yellow dandelions. She must have looked hard to find them because there aren't many around now that it's October.

'Will they do?'

The dandelions are a bit small and shabby, but I don't want to hurt her feelings.

'Perfect.' I lie back.

There is a pause. 'What now?' asks Mae.

'I think you have to say some sad words,' I say, my eyes closing again. These chairs are very comfy.

Mae takes a breath and begins a speech. 'Oh, sweet Lady of Shalott. You were always . . . um . . . in your tower. Spinning all day.'

'She did weaving,' I say sleepily.

'Weaving all day,' corrects Mae. 'Never looking out of the window in case the curse should come upon you. Until that fateful day . . .'

Her voice is soothing and the air is warm, and I'm soft and comfortable. It's very peaceful until . . .

'WOOOOOO!!'

My eyes jerk open and I sit up, disorientated.

Christopher is standing in the doorway, arms out like a zombie, draped in a white sheet. 'RAAARGH!' he adds, lurching towards us.

Mae and I watch, unimpressed.

'What are you meant to be?' asks Mae. 'Because if you're trying to be a ghost, they don't say "RAARGH" and zombies don't go "WOOO", and neither of them wears a white sheet, so it looks like you're having an identity crisis.'

Christopher pulls the sheet off his head and scowls at us. 'Both,' he says. 'A ghost zombie.'

'Technically,' I say, 'they're both dead, so you couldn't get a ghost zombie, because it'd be like being dead twice over, and that's not possible.'

Christopher huffs. 'Yeah? I can do what I like on Halloween. Ghost zombies are cool. Mum's going to make it into a proper costume for me. And it was way better than what you were doing, anyway, Sleeping Beauty.'

'I was not being Sleeping Beauty,' I say, feeling my face go pink. 'That's a stupid story. I was being the Lady of Shalott.'

He stares at me. 'The who?'

'Oh, go away and be a child somewhere else,' says Mae in an impressively patronising manner.

He sticks his tongue out and disappears. We hear him singing as he thumps up the stairs: 'Calypso's being a *princess*, Calypso's being a *princess* . . .'

Mae sighs. 'I'm so sorry, he's such an idiot.' She turns to me. 'Are you going out trick-or-treating at Halloween? You could come with us, if you like.'

'Oh, um . . . I haven't got a costume.'

Mae says pleadingly, 'I've got a cat and a witch costume, so you could have one, and we can pretend we don't know Christopher.'

'I've never been trick-or-treating,' I admit. 'We live too far out, so no one ever comes to our house. Where do you go?'

'Oh, not far,' Mae says. 'Back at our old house we just went to the people we knew in our street. Dad usually comes with us and hides round the corner.'

I am not sure. 'Can I think about it? I'll ask my dad.' Though I know what he'll say. He'll say it's an American tradition that's unpleasant and commercial. Knocking on people's doors at night and asking them for sweets isn't good manners. Not that I can say that to Mae. We're the very best of friends, but in many ways we're still very different. And it sounds like her dad doesn't mind being American and commercial.

Mae grins. 'Beg him to let you come.' She glances at the pushed-together chairs in the middle of the room. 'I guess we've finished doing *The Lady of Shalott*, haven't we? No ghost zombies in that poem.'

I laugh. 'No. Can you imagine? The Lady looks out of the window to see a white figure with its arms out . . .' I raise my arms as Christopher had done. '"Wooo!" cried the Lady of Shalott!' Then I notice that Mae's smile has frozen and her face has turned pale. 'Mae? What's the matter?'

Her mouth forms an 'o' shape, but no sound comes out.

'What?' I look in the same direction as her gaze. 'Oh, I forgot I was still holding the dandelions.' They're squashed and sticky now, and there are brown marks on my hands where the stems have leaked dandelion milk. 'Ew. Gross.'

'The fabric.' Mae bites her lip and says in a whisper, 'Look.'

I am draped in the beautiful satin brocade: the thick, heavily embroidered material that must have cost a fortune. I look down – and the kingfisher blue is spotted and splodged with brown stains, just like my hands.

'Oh no,' I whisper. 'Oh no.'

That beautiful fabric. Surely the nicest of all the material – and we promised not to spoil it or get it dirty. We promised.

What will Mae's mum say?

13

We promised to be careful. And the fabric is so, so beautiful. Mae's mum probably bought it in some exotic country, from a seller in a bazaar – we won't be able to replace it.

I start to tremble. For one brief, insane moment I consider running out of the house and never coming back. Never owning up, leaving Mae to do it. Never seeing the disappointed, angry look on her mother's face.

But I don't, of course. Because that would be cowardly, and I am not a coward. So I carefully wade to the French doors, not touching anything, and place the crumpled dandelions on the step outside. Then Mae helps unwind me from the fabric and I go to wash my hands. They stop being sticky but the brown stains don't come off. My heart sinks lower. If I can't get my hands clean, how will we ever get the fabric clean?

'Maybe we should try to wash it,' Mae whispers at my ear. She is clutching the brocade.

'No,' I say. 'We'd only make it worse. And the colour might run or something. We have to find your mum.' My voice wobbles.

Mae's mum is in the kitchen, chopping carrots. She turns with a smile but sees our faces. 'What is it?'

I step forward. 'I'm so sorry,' I say. 'There was an accident.'

Mae holds out the kingfisher brocade.

'It's dandelions,' I say. 'I mean, it's dandelion milk, from the stems. They leaked. I was being the Lady of Shalott and we needed some flowers. I forgot they would leak. And now . . .' I swallow.

Mae's mum washes her hands and then comes to take the fabric from Mae. She looks very serious. She examines the brown stains and takes a deep breath. 'Oh dear,' she says.

I feel tears spring to my eyes and I bite my lip.

'It's in the middle too,' says Mae's mum, stretching out the fabric and checking all along its length. 'So it's not even a question of cutting off one end. Oh, girls.' The disappointment in her voice cuts me to the quick.

Mae bursts into tears. 'We're so sorry, Mummy! We were trying so hard not to damage anything!'

Her mother sighs. 'I know. It's all right. I mean, it's not, because this is some of my favourite fabric, and I was saving it for something very special. But there's nothing to be done.'

'Can it . . .' I say in a quiver. 'Can it . . . be washed?'

She gives a sad smile. 'No, not really. This kind of fabric doesn't wash well, and dandelion stains require a chemical treatment. It would destroy it.'

'Oh.' I can't help it. A tear rolls down my cheek. 'I'm sorry. If I . . . need to pay . . .' I have no idea what I'm saying. I don't even have pocket money. How would I pay for something like this?

Mae is sobbing so hard she sounds like she might be sick. And it infects me: suddenly the tears are streaming down my face like a waterfall, and although I'm not making a sound I can't speak any more, and everything is blurred.

Mae's mum puts down the fabric and holds out her arms, and Mae steps into them without hesitation. But only one arm folds around her. The other is still held out to me.

I step forward too, and then I am enveloped in

warmth and security and strength, and the tears stream even faster because it's almost like I'm borrowing a mother, just for a few moments. Something deep inside me bursts and my knees buckle, but Mae's mum holds me up.

Someone else is holding me up. I don't have to hold myself up, for this moment. I don't need my own inner strength, because someone else is being strong for me.

It is such a relief.

14

Mae's mum forgives us. For those few moments before she hugged us, I tried to persuade myself that I wouldn't mind being on my own again, best-friendless, independent and solitary. I've spent years practising it; I can do it again, can't I?

But knowing I don't have to, knowing that I'm forgiven and that I can still play with Mae and spend time with her family, makes me cry again with relief. And it makes me feel even more part of Mae's family – more accepted for being me.

I go round to their house every day during half term. Though I try not to have dinner there because I worry that my dad won't remember to eat if I'm not back. Mae's family does so much together that I find myself automatically trying to get Dad to do stuff with me too. It's difficult, though; he has a lot of work to do and he doesn't seem to have time even to play Scrabble with me or go for a walk.

His response when I ask him about trick-or-treating is exactly what I expected. 'No, Calypso, I don't approve of it.'

'But I'd be with Mae,' I say, 'and Christopher – and her dad will be there too.'

He shakes his head. 'I don't like the tradition. And coming home with a bucket-load of sweets is not good for you.'

I wouldn't mind, I think to myself. I've never had a bucket-load of sweets before. 'Please, Dad . . .' It's funny. I didn't really want to go, but now that he's said no, I sort of do.

'You can decorate a pumpkin if you like,' he says. 'That's harmless enough.' Then he goes into his library and shuts the door. The conversation is over.

I stand in the hallway alone and look at the floor. Am I angry? Disappointed? Relieved? Is it possible to be all of those things at once?

Mae is simply disappointed. 'Did you tell him my dad would be coming too?'

'Yes. He still says no.'

She pulls a face. 'Your dad can be a bit . . . um . . .'

'A bit what?'

She shuffles awkwardly. 'A bit . . . Well, does he do any fun things, ever?'

I open my mouth to say yes, of course. He's offered to carve a pumpkin with me (actually, did he? Or am I supposed to do it myself?); he can make a game out of emptying kitchen cupboards to find food; he takes me out for pizza on a whim . . .

For once, my words desert me. 'Oh,' I say uncomfortably, 'he can be fun. He just has a lot of work to do.'

On the last Saturday of half term, Mae and I have our first session in our writing den. It's not finished by any means, but the floor is no longer damp and we've painted the walls inside. Mae's dad has found a piece of leftover carpet and cut it to the right size, so it's quite comfortable. The day isn't too chilly, so we reckon we can work in there for at least an hour before we get cold. Mae and I shut the little door and smile at each other in our own space with curtains and cushions. It's going to be wonderful in the summer.

'I've brought my Halloween sweets,' she says, holding up a paper bag decorated with pumpkins.

'I wish you'd come with us – we'd have got twice as many!' She hands over a lollipop. 'Sugar is good for thinking.'

'Thanks,' I say, sticking the lollipop in my mouth and opening the hardback notebook. 'Let's get started.'

We've been working hard on our story. It now runs to twenty-two pages and has developed way beyond my initial idea of the girl who has survived a nuclear war. We invented an area of France that was unaffected by the radiation because it's under huge domes, like the Eden Project in Cornwall. Our central character, Persephone, or Sephy for short, has to travel through dangerous waters to get there, stealing a boat and nearly being eaten by sharks. We have to invent new sharks because there aren't really sharks in the English Channel, but they're necessary for the drama in the story.

What's even more exciting is that Mae has learned how to upload a book to the internet. It doesn't seem all that hard. We have a test practice with the first chapter of *After Armageddon*, our epic story. 'Armageddon' means the battle to end the world, so our title is actually quite clever. Mae persuades her mum to set up the account in her name, because you have to be over eighteen. I'm so excited when Mae shows it to me, actually on a real website. We use a photograph of a dark wood that Mae's mum took as the cover design and set the price at fifty pence, because it's very short, and we wait impatiently for two days to see if anyone will buy it. No one does.

'We need to do publicity for it,' says Mae, trying to reassure me. 'It's only because no one knows it's there. We should send messages to people asking them to buy our book. Maybe we could do adverts too.'

I'm not sure I want to learn how to do publicity things. I just like writing the stories. I begin to wonder whether putting our story online is really worth the effort. But then Mae comes to school a couple of days later beaming all over her face.

'Someone's bought it!' she says.

'No!' I say. 'You're making it up!'

But she isn't. There, in our account, a payment is showing. I feel a rush of euphoria. We are proper writers!

'I hope they enjoy it,' I say, feeling so proud that I want to tell everyone at school.

'Of course they will,' Mae says. 'They'll probably

write a review saying they can't wait to read the rest of the book.'

I am so thrilled that I burst into Dad's study that day after school to tell him.

'Dad!' I say. 'You'll never guess!'

I have chosen a bad moment. The computer is on and he is glaring at the screen.

'Not now, Calypso,' he says, without glancing at me. 'I'm working. This blasted editor doesn't know what he's talking about.'

'But Dad!' I say again. 'I'm a published author!'

That gets his attention. His head snaps round. 'What did you say?'

'I'm a published author,' I say. 'Well, sort of. Mae and I put a story we wrote online and someone has bought it!'

He stares at me for what seems like too long a moment. He shakes his head slightly. 'What do you mean, someone bought it?' His voice is odd.

I want to pull up a chair to his desk but there isn't another one in here, so I perch on the very edge.

'Mae learned how to do it on the computer,' I say, glancing at his. The email from the editor is on screen, and there seems to be a long list of bullet points. 'We're writing this story together, and we wanted to see if we could do it properly, you know – sell it. So we put the first chapter on a website where people can buy digital books, and someone's bought it! It's only fifty pence – it's not much, but it works, and maybe when the story is finished, millions of people will buy it and we'll be rich! And I can have a computer of my own, and we could buy a new car, and we could go on holiday! In fact' – my mouth runs on by itself – 'we could go *abroad*! And we could even get a *housekeeper*! To do the cleaning!' I stop, panting, alight with my vision of the future.

Then I see my father's face.

'What's the matter?'

He looks like he has a pain, his eyebrows are pulled so tightly together, and his lips are pale.

'Are you all right?'

He seems unable to speak. His cheeks are making funny shapes, like he's clenching his teeth together at the back. And there's a kind of low grunting.

He finally growls out, 'You put a story online? And someone has *paid* for it? Not – not a publisher?'

'Oh – no!' I say with a laugh. 'No, no, nothing like that. We just put our story up and someone downloaded it. To their computer or their phone or something. They paid fifty pence to be able to do it. It's not a publishing thing really. But we've sort of published it ourselves by putting it there. You know?'

There is a long silence. It dawns on me that he doesn't understand a word. Dad lives on paper. What Mae and I have done is as alien as inventing a hovercar.

The pleasure I had taken earlier from the knowledge of our first sale ebbs away. The warmth of knowing we were achieving something I had longed for is cold.

'Anyway,' I say eventually, getting down from the desk and rubbing the part of my thigh that has gone numb, 'I just wanted to tell you. I'll – um – I'll go do my homework now.' As I reach the door, I ask, 'Do you want a cup of tea?'

But he's staring at the place on his desk where I was sitting and he's as still as a statue. He doesn't look angry. He looks pained, as though he's remembering a very bad memory, or as though he's just watched a terrible accident. I bite my lip. I must have made him feel bad, though I don't know how. As I turn away, something registers in my mind, and I whip round. There are tears in his eyes. Definite tears.

I go straight to my room and sit on my bed, trembling. Outside, I can hear the pops and squeals of fireworks as Bonfire Night begins, but I don't even glance out of the window.

My father doesn't cry. Ever. I must have done something very, very bad indeed.

15

Things get even worse at school the next day. I can see it in Mae's face: her lips quiver and her eyes are shiny with tears.

'What is it?' I ask, dreading the response.

She pulls my arm and takes me to a corner of the classroom. We don't usually sit here, and someone will be along in a moment to demand we get out of their seat. *Anne of Green Gables* plays through my mind: the scene where Anne has a disastrous tea party and is forbidden to be friends with Diana.

I clasp Mae's hand. 'What's happened?' I ask in a desperate whisper. 'You look *distraught*. Are we to be parted?' A new juddering thought hits me. 'Mae, are you dying from cancer?'

Am I going to lose her like I lost my mother? The breath stops in my lungs.

'Worse,' says Mae, and she swallows. 'We've had a review.'

'A what?'

'A review. From the person who bought our story.'

It takes me a moment to understand her. At first I am swept with cleansing relief. She doesn't have cancer! We are not to be parted!

'What kind of review?'

'A really bad one.' Tears run down her face. 'Oh, Calypso, she said some *awful* things.'

'What kind of things?'

'She said it wasn't worth the fifty pence. She said it was badly written and that it was five minutes of her life she'd never get back. She said it looked like it had been written by three-year-olds . . .' Mae is hiccupping now.

I feel cold and sick again. 'That's horrible.'

'I didn't want to tell you,' she says. 'I tried to delete it, but the website wouldn't let me. Oh, Calypso! No one will buy it if they read that review!'

'We'll take it down,' I say firmly. 'We'll take our chapter off the site so the review goes too. Then we'll work on the complete story until it's perfect before we put it up.'

'I'm not sure we should now,' Mae says miserably. 'What if people don't like the full story?'

'You can't please everyone,' I say. 'Besides, it's only our first book. We're learning all the time. The second one will be better, and the third one better still.'

'I was thinking we should give up writing.' Mae is despondent.

'Don't be silly,' I tell her, though I am frightened by this. I look forward to our writing sessions. Without her, I'd have to go back to doing it by myself, and I've learned it's a lot more fun with two.

We can't talk any more because we are kicked out of our seats by two irate classmates, and the lesson begins.

Mae shows me the review at lunchtime on a library computer and I see what she means.

Had I realised that this was a mere 500 words, I wouldn't have wasted my money or my time. In fact, even if it were free, I wouldn't recommend that anyone reads it. After Armageddon *is an over-ambitious title by two authors who clearly have ideas beyond their ability. The writing is childish and clunky, the plot ridiculous and the characters boring. It took me five minutes to read it – five minutes I'll never get back. Five minutes I could have spent more productively on the toilet or cleaning up after the cat. It looks like it's been written by three-year-olds and is an example of why self-publishing can be a really bad idea.*

I stare at the screen, at the spiteful, vindictive words.

'Wow,' I say. 'She really hates it.' There's a hot, tight feeling in my stomach. It's like I'm on the edge of an extreme reaction and I can choose which way to go.

It's a book review. It's not cancer, or being parted from friends. It's nothing. I let the feeling bubble up and out of me and I laugh and I laugh.

'She *really* hates it!' I whoop. 'She could have been on the *toilet*!'

Mr Simmons comes over, looking concerned. 'Is everything all right?' he asks. He can't tell if I'm laughing or crying.

'It's fine!' I shriek. 'We're fine! We got a bad review!'

Mae is staring at me like I'm a lunatic.

Mr Simmons smiles in relief. 'You seem to be taking it well.'

For some reason this makes me laugh even more. My stomach hurts and I cross my arms over it.

'Calm down, Calypso,' says Mae. She sounds alarmed.

I try. Returning to normality after that level of giggles is hard to do and it takes me a long time. Even after five minutes, I still get that after-giggle reflex, the one that makes you chuckle out of nowhere for a moment. Mr Simmons goes back to his desk, shaking his head in bafflement.

Mae hasn't laughed at all. 'Calypso, that was really weird. Are you okay?'

'My dad hates that word,' I confide in her. 'I love it. Okay, okay, okay! It's like an echo!'

'Calypso . . .'

'Oh, Mae, it's all right. I'm fine – I'm okay, remember?' I give another giggle. 'You know how sometimes you've got to laugh otherwise you'd cry? This is that. One of those. Come on. Switch the thing off. Let's not think about it for the moment.'

'Okay . . .' says Mae slowly. She logs out of our account, and shuts down the browser, casting slightly worried glances at me on and off. 'When you did that . . . it kind of freaked me out a bit. Are you back to normal now?'

'Normal?' I say, feeling strangely light-headed. 'I've never been *normal*, didn't you know that? No one in my family has ever been normal. My dad definitely isn't normal. Who writes about *lemons*, for goodness' sake? And my mum wasn't normal either. She was an artist. She painted landscapes and skies, but she also painted pictures of things you can't see. There's one in the attic called *Despair*. It's just black and red and grey with tiny pinpricks in the canvas. And she did another one called *Happiness*, which is just yellow all over. With glitter sprinkles. I mean, even *I* could've painted that. It was in an exhibition at the National Gallery once, and people said it was amazing. But it's completely crazy.' An idea strikes me. 'Listen, why don't you come home with me today after school? Come and see my house. I could take you up into the attic to show you Mum's paintings!'

Mae is definitely alarmed. 'Not today, Calypso. Besides, how would I get there?'

'On the bus with me!' I say with enthusiasm. Suddenly, this is the best idea I've ever had. 'Come on, it'll be fun! We can sneak you on, hide you under my seat!' I'm in danger of losing myself in the giggles again.

Mae stands up, pushing her chair back so sharply that it falls over. 'No. Stop it. You're being all weird. I'm going back to class.'

Oh no – I've done something wrong. 'Mae, don't go!' I plead. I grab for my bag, tangling the strap in the legs of my chair and nearly tripping up. In the time it takes me to detangle it, she's gone. I feel panicky. What happened? I race after her, Mr Simmons calling out in a warning tone something that I don't hear.

Mae doesn't talk to me for the rest of the day, and after a while I give up trying.

I go home on my own on the school bus.

16

Dad is in his library when I get back. Of course he is – he's always there. The euphoric and crazy feeling I had earlier has gone and now I just feel so very tired. What if Mae never speaks to me again? I don't think I could bear it.

I don't want to go straight to my room. I don't want to be on my own. So instead, I knock on the library door.

Dad grunts, 'Come in!'

His desk is piled high with A4 envelopes stuffed to bursting. He is writing laboriously on each one, referring to a notebook in between.

'Hi,' I say, surprised. 'What's this?'

'This,' says Dad, grinning from ear to ear, 'is my manuscript. Printed and bound and ready to be sent to publishers!'

My eyebrows climb so far up my forehead they

feel like they're buried in my head.

'Wow,' I say. 'Wow.' I am shocked. I can't tell him that I never really believed it would be finished, much less ever leave the house. 'You did it.'

'I know.' He beams at me. 'We're both going to be published!'

'Actually,' I say, 'that's gone kind of bad.'

He doesn't look angry or sad any more, but kind of interested, so I tell him about the awful review.

'Oh, Calypso,' he says, sounding genuinely sympathetic. 'I'm so sorry. Some people are needlessly unpleasant.'

He's so kind about it that I feel tearful. I gulp back the lump in my throat out of habit.

'She didn't need to be so nasty,' I say. 'She could have said it wasn't her kind of thing and left it at that.'

He shrugs. 'Some people make themselves feel better by saying malicious things to others. I've never understood it myself. Putting down other people should not make you feel superior. It should make you feel ashamed.' He smiles at me. 'Shall we go out for dinner?'

'I'd love to,' I say, 'but I'm really tired. I don't think I want anything to eat.'

'Nonsense.' He sends me up to have a bath and

then he brings me cheese on toast in bed, with a mug of hot chocolate. Not only that, he sits by my bed and reads to me, from Homer's *Odyssey*. It makes me feel like a little girl again, when he and Mum used to take it in turns to put me to bed and read to me. Mum read things like *Winnie-the-Pooh* and *The Gruffalo*. Dad read Kipling's *Just So Stories* and *The Jungle Book*.

I feel soft and sleepy and comfortable. I even tell Dad about my strange reaction in the library and how Mae stopped talking to me. He nods as though he understands and takes my plate and mug downstairs.

When he comes back, he says, 'I rang Mae's mum. She said Mae was sorry about how she behaved this afternoon.'

'Oh!' I feel even warmer at the thought.

'I think you frightened Mae a bit. She said you were – wild.' He sounds puzzled by the word. 'What do you think caused it?'

'I don't know,' I say. 'It felt like I was bursting. Like I couldn't stop it, even though I wanted to.'

He nods again and says, 'Did you invite Mae here?'

I feel embarrassed. 'Yes. Sort of. I was telling her about Mum's paintings . . .' I trail off. 'She doesn't have to come. I should have asked you first.'

He shakes his head. 'It's fine. It's all arranged. Her mum's going to bring both of you here tomorrow after school and come and pick up Mae at five.'

My heart thumps. Mae is coming here! 'Thanks, Dad. That's brilliant.'

He gazes at me for a minute. 'You're welcome. I'm sorry if things have been a bit rough for you lately. I've taken on some more proofreading, now that I have more time again. So there'll be a bit more money. For food and – clothes and things. Do you need shoes or something?'

'My school shoes are quite tight.'

'There you are. We'll go and buy some shoes at the weekend.'

'Thanks, Dad.' My eyelids are so heavy they're closing by themselves. Fuzzily, I see him switch off the lamp and blur into the gloom as the door closes.

17

I am crazily excited about the idea of Mae coming to my house, but I hide it because I don't want to frighten her again. Looking back, I'm not really quite sure what happened there in the library. Wild, Mae said. I've never been wild before. It felt very strange – terrifying and exciting all at the same time.

But today I feel more optimistic and *so happy* that my best friend is coming to my house. Mae is back to her normal self too and we have a big hug to make up.

'I'm really sorry,' I tell her.

She nods. 'It's okay. Mum said maybe you were just really tired. When people are tired they do strange things.'

The day drags at school, the way it does when you're looking forward to the end of it. When Miss

Spotlin finally lets us out, I am so eager to leave that I forget my book bag and she has to call me back.

'Going somewhere exciting?' she asks with a smile.

'Just home,' I say happily. 'With Mae. Mae's coming round.'

She nods, the smile becoming warmer. 'I'm very glad to hear it. You've become a different person since you made such a good friend.'

The words spin around my head as I push my way outside. A *different* person. Am I different since I met Mae? I don't feel any different inside – or do I? I'm still *me*, but maybe I'm just a bit . . . happier?

Actually, I'm a *lot* happier. Mae has filled a gap I didn't even know was there.

She takes my hand as we walk to the school gates to find her mum's car, and my heart begins to sing. *Mae's coming home with me. Mae's coming home with me . . .*

In the car, squashed between Mae and Christopher, I feel worries resurface.

'My house isn't like yours,' I say to Mae. 'I hope you won't be cold. And it's not as tidy. You don't have to take off your shoes because we haven't got nice carpets like yours.'

Mae smiles. 'I'm sure it's fine. Anyway, you've got a library. I don't have a library.'

'That's true.' I feel a little better, and when the car pulls up at my house, I almost push Mae out in my eagerness.

Mae's mum smiles and says, 'Have fun, girls. I'll be back at five, okay?'

'Okay!' I say cheerfully. Then I take Mae up the front path to the door and open it with my key.

'It's so cool that you have your own front-door key,' she says in admiration as we wave her mum off.

I feel quite sophisticated.

'Dad!' I call as I shut the front door and the hallway is plunged into gloom. 'We're home!'

There's no answer, but that's not surprising.

'He's probably deep in some manuscript,' I say. 'What do you want to do first?'

'Wow,' says Mae, looking around with wide eyes. 'It's like something out of a book.'

I gaze around too. Our front hallway has little black and white tiles in a pattern that's long been cracked and chipped. The stairs rise from the floor, uncarpeted, the wooden slats sloping unevenly towards the landing. Mum's painting, the one of the field, is back on the wall, and I switch on the overhead light so that I can show Mae.

'This is one of my mum's paintings,' I say, and feel a swell of pride.

Mae gazes at the painting.

'You can't really see it properly,' I add, 'because the light is too dim.'

'It's beautiful,' she says. 'Your mum was really talented.'

My stomach warms at her praise. My mum *was* talented.

'It makes me want to cry a bit, it's so beautiful,' she says.

I beam. This is the highest possible praise from Mae.

'Through there is the kitchen,' I say, waving my arm at the darkness behind the staircase.

'Can I see your library? The one that's just for you?'

'Of course!' I bound up the stairs, taking them two at a time. 'Follow me!'

Mae lets out a little gasp when I push open the box-room door. Three sides of the room are filled with bookshelves, and the shelves are all full, some of them two deep in books.

'Are these all yours?' she breathes in awe.

'Yes,' I say. 'Though most of them came from my mum – she had them when she was little.' I run to my room and fetch the photograph from my bedside table.

Mae smiles at it. 'She's very beautiful. Her hair is gorgeous.'

'I'm hoping mine goes like that when I'm older,' I tell her.

'You look so like her,' says Mae, handing back the photo.

'Really?' I feel a glow of pride. 'She loved books, just like us. She collected loads of them. I've got some in here, her children's books. The grown-up ones are downstairs, in my dad's library. They're waiting for me to be old enough to read them.'

Mae sniffs. 'Is there . . . what can I smell?'

'Mum's oil paints,' I say. 'This used to be her studio. She went to art school in Paris.'

'Do you paint too?' Mae asks.

I shake my head. 'Not really. I kind of like words better.'

She nods and starts to read along the shelves. '*The Wizard of Oz*, *The Secret World of Polly Flint*, *The Little White Horse* . . . I haven't even heard of some of these!'

'Borrow any you like,' I say enthusiastically. I sit down on the floor next to her. 'We've got some really old annuals from years and years ago too, like 1980. Look.'

Mae pulls one out at random. '*Judy*,' she says. 'Wow, look at the cartoons in here! Oh – it's about ballet! I've never seen a comic about ballet.' Her eyes start to follow the strip across the page.

I wish you could bottle feelings, so that you could take them out at other times when you needed them. At that moment, my feelings would have filled several bottles with sparkly red, pink and orange swirls of happiness. Mae is here, in my house, in my library, in the room that used to be my mother's, and it's like there's magic around us. I can almost *feel* my mum here with us – through her books and the smell of her paints. I just know she would like Mae. We sit on the floor together, pulling out books and exclaiming over words and pictures until I lose track of the time.

Mae says softly, 'I would swap my laptop for your library.'

I smile. 'It's my special place.'

'What's the other one like?' she asks. 'Your dad's library?'

I get to my feet. 'I'll show you!'

She looks nervous. 'Won't he mind?'

I beam at her. 'I'm sure it'll be okay. And we can look at Mum's other books too.' Having shared these books, the photograph, the painting with Mae, I want to share more of Mum's things. 'Come on!'

I bound down the stairs, Mae following more carefully behind me.

'Dad!' I call. 'We're coming in, all right?'

There is no answer, so I push open the heavy door to the library anyway.

'Oh!' Dad isn't here. I blink, taken aback. He's always here. Where could he have gone?

The pile of A4 envelopes on the desk has gone. A small book of stamps, most of them removed, sits forlornly alone. Of course. He's gone to the post office.

'Your dad went out without telling you?' asks Mae, sounding disapproving.

'He probably left me a note somewhere,' I say airily. 'I think he's gone to the post office, to post his manuscripts off to publishers.'

'Ah!' Mae's expression clears. 'So he won't be long then.'

'No, I shouldn't think so.' I go to the middle of the room and do a kind of twirl. 'What do you think?'

Mae stares at the shelves. 'They look very old. Why have they got doors on them?'

'Shutters. To protect them from sunlight,' I explain. 'Look over here.' I show her the conservatory-greenhouse thing through the French windows.

Mae's eyes widen. 'Are those lemons? Growing on trees?'

'Yes!' I unlock the door and we step into the greenhouse. The heady scent of lemons is intoxicating, and the air feels warmer than the rest of the house.

Mae reaches out to a ripening lemon in awe. 'I didn't know – I mean, I knew lemons grew on trees, but I didn't realise you could grow them in this country.'

'You have to keep them warm,' I say, proud of my father's obsession for once. 'We'll bring them into the house when the temperature gets to freezing. But the greenhouse traps sunlight, so they're all right for now. They're lovely, aren't they?'

'Amazing. We've got a conservatory at my house,' Mae says. 'Do you think I could grow a lemon tree too?'

'Why not?' I say. 'When Dad comes back, you can ask him. He knows everything there is to know about lemons.'

She smiles. 'That would be brilliant!'

We step back into the library and I lock the door. 'What kind of books does your dad have, then?' asks Mae, looking at the shuttered shelves.

'Oh, they're mostly very old,' I tell her. 'You know, hardbacks with dust jackets. Dickens and the Bible and stuff. Encyclopaedias and dictionaries and old atlases. He's got lots of travel and biography books too. Anything that mentions lemons, you see, for research.' I grin. 'But they're not as interesting as Mum's books. Her shelf is over here, I think. I'll show you.'

I click the little bolt at the base of one of the shutters. It concertinas back easily, surprising me. I remembered them being stiff.

And then the breath stops in my throat, and my brain slows to a halt, and Mae gasps, a tiny sound.

'Where are the books?' she whispers.

And I stare and stare and don't know what to say. Where once there were rows and rows of books – Mum's books – now there are none. Instead, in their place, there are lemons.

Row upon row of lemons. Some are shiny and waxy, freshly picked; others look shrivelled and as hard as rock. I pull back another shutter, and another and another, until all of the shelves are uncovered.

No books, only lemons.

A library of lemons.

18

I stand and stare at the open cupboards. Lemons instead of books. *Lemons.*

Mae is making a funny panting sound, almost like she wants to laugh, but is horrified at the same time. 'Did you *know*?' she whispers.

I am ashamed. So ashamed that a big part of me wants to giggle and say, 'Of course I knew! There were never any books in here! It's all a big joke! A lemony joke!' But there is dust in my throat along with the citrus tang, and I can't utter a word. My mind is empty, refusing to believe it. My eyes are dry because I haven't blinked since I saw the shelves.

And then there is a snick-snack sound, and I know the front door is opening. And there are footsteps in the hall, and the rustle of a coat being hung up. I try to swallow, but nothing happens because my throat has stuck, and Mae's panting gets faster – and then Dad comes in.

I have never been frightened of my father, but as I turn to look at him I feel a deep terror. How could he have been doing this and I never knew? What kind of madness is this?

He sees the shutters thrown back on the shelves, the yellow rows exposed. He sees Mae and then me, and there is something in his eyes, like he *knows* he's been found out and is trying to decide what to do next.

After a long second of silence, he smiles and says, 'Good afternoon, you two. I'm sorry I wasn't in when you came home from school. Did you have a good day?'

His voice sounds perfectly ordinary. For a moment I am almost fooled into thinking that I have dreamed all this. But then I reach out to touch a lemon, and it is *real*.

'Where are the books, Dad?' I say, in a voice that cracks.

'The books?' He licks his lips nervously.

'The books that were on these shelves. Where are they?' My voice is growing stronger, and there is something steely forming inside me, like tiny splashes of molten metal gliding towards each other to solidify into a lead lump.

'I . . . er . . . well, I didn't need them any more.'

Mae is frozen, like a statue, only her eyes flicking from side to side.

'You didn't need them?' I repeat. 'The Dickens, the Jane Austen? The Sherlock Holmes, the Thomas Hardy?' My brain is stuttering, like a car when it won't start. '*The Atlas of the World*, all the volumes of the *Encyclopaedia Britannica*? *Mum's* books – the ones you were saving for me when I'm older?' I feel my throat closing on the words, and I force more air into my lungs. 'Where did they go?' I ask, more loudly. 'What did you do with them?'

Dad is pale, pale as a ghost. 'Look, Calypso,' he says, 'I needed the space, for my lemons.' He lifts an arm to gesture towards the shelves. His mouth lifts in a half-smile. 'You see?'

'*The books, Dad.*' My jaw is tense.

'The books are behind the shed.'

'The shed?' I say, bewildered. 'The *garden* shed?'

'Yes. Behind the shed.'

'They're *outside*?' I can't process his words.

'They're in boxes,' he says defensively, but his eyes are guilty.

‘But it’s wet out there!’ I can’t remember the last time I went into the garden shed, much less looked behind it. ‘When did you do this? How long have they been out there?’ The lead lump in my stomach is growing heavier, and my jaw aches with anger, and I don’t wait for his answer. ‘How could you do that? They’ll be ruined!’ Mum’s books! The books that were meant to be mine!

‘But – my lemons . . .’ Dad waves a hand to the shelves. ‘They’re an important part of my research. You understand? I needed –’

‘No!’ I shout. ‘No, I don’t understand! How can lemons be more important than books?’ My voice rises. ‘Books are everything! You should know that – you helped me build my own library! Books give us questions and answers and friends and magic! My *mother’s* books were in here, Dad! Things she loved, pieces of her! Pieces of her that were meant to be *mine*! And you’ve just chucked them away, to be rained on and eaten by rats?’ I am screaming. ‘They’re *books*! These are just *lemons*! How can you even *think* . . .?’ I can hear the words coming out of my mouth and I want to laugh because they sound so crazy. But I am so, so angry.

I grab a lemon from the nearest shelf, feel its weight in my hand.

Dad takes a short step forward, his arm out. 'Leave it, Calypso, please –'

I throw it at him. It hits him on the arm and he flinches. The lemon was old and shrivelled. It will probably leave a bruise. Well, good. I grab another lemon, and another and another, and I throw them at the floor, the walls, his desk. One makes a dent in the door – it's as hard as a stone. Another bounces off the computer screen, making it rock on its stand. Some of them split on impact, releasing grey mould like tiny sneezes.

Soon the room is covered in burst lemons, and the air is full of the smell of rotten and decaying fruit. But still, like a recurring nightmare, there are more lemons on the shelves.

Mae claps her hands to her mouth and runs out of the room.

I cannot stop myself, and no one tries to stop me, and so I throw and throw until the shelves are empty, but I am still so angry that there is nothing left to do but shout.

'Where are the books?' I scream. 'What have you been *doing*?'

I know the answers, of course, but there is nothing else I can shout. What kind of person throws away books and keeps rotten lemons on bookshelves? I shout at him over and over, using words I've never used before, words that strike and slice and stab. They pour out of me like poison from an unstoppered bottle. I can no more hold them back than I can stop breathing. They tear through me and set upon my father, who makes no sound, does not fight back, gives me nothing.

When there are no more words left to say, I simply stand and stare at my father. He looks smaller, somehow. And a bit yellow and shrivelled, like one of his horrible lemons. He has been looking at the ground, but now in the silence he glances up at me. I can see that he is frightened. Frightened of me. Right now, I'm frightened of me too.

'I'm so sorry, Calypso,' he whispers. 'I didn't know what I was doing.'

It is like the air has been sucked out of my lungs. I feel so wobbly that I have to sit down on the floor.

What is he talking about? How can my father not know what he's doing?

He sits down too, amid the mess. Five metres apart, we sit silently, until the doorbell rings.

Mae must have been waiting for it, because I hear footsteps immediately afterwards. What time is it? Surely it's too early for her mum to collect her?

There is a murmur of voices in the hall, and Mae sounds like she's crying. I feel bad. I should go and talk to her, but I feel so heavy I can't move. And how can I explain this?

I hear Mae's mum come in, though I can't move my head to look at her.

'Goodness,' she says in a friendly way, 'what a mess in here. Let's see what we can do to sort it out.'

From the corner of my eye I see her bend down to my father. 'Hello,' she says. 'I'm Mae's mum, Aiko. I've come to help.' Her voice sounds absurdly normal, like this kind of thing happens every day.

I hear him mutter something. I am gazing at a lemon on the floor. It hasn't split; it's not old and shrivelled. It's completely undamaged. Shiny and yellow, and I just know that it is fresh and juicy inside. It's perfect.

It's a few minutes more before Mae's mum comes over to me. 'Hello, Calypso,' she says. 'Listen, why don't you come back to our house this evening? You could have a sleepover with Mae.'

My neck creaks as I turn my head to look at her. I feel sore and stiff. Exhausted. 'It was a library of lemons,' I say.

Tears run down my face, which surprises me. I didn't know they were coming.

'He threw away the books,' I whisper, my voice tight again.

'I know,' she says gently. 'Don't worry, we'll find them. We'll fix it.'

'Can you fix my dad?' I ask. *What's wrong with him?*

She pauses for a moment. 'One step at a time,' she says, which isn't really an answer.

I let her help me up, and we walk past my father, back to the doorway, where Mae is standing with a worried expression.

'Calypso's going to come back with us,' says her mum. 'So I'll go upstairs with her and pack a few things for an overnight bag.'

'I'll come too,' says Mae quickly.

I don't blame her. My father is still sitting on the floor of the library, and who wants to be alone with a crazy person and a room that stinks of lemons?

Mae's mum packs for me. I sit on the bed and do nothing. She keeps up a cheerful chatter as she works. The noise is strangely soothing and some of the small, jagged pieces in my head start to melt away.

When my bag is stuffed, we go back downstairs and out of the front door. I climb into their car – the nice, warm, biscuity-smelling car; the one that starts first time, every time – and I click in the seat belt. Mae sits by the other window, casting anxious sideways glances at me.

As we drive to Mae's house it starts to rain.

19

It's hard to explain how I feel because I'm not sure I know myself. Part of me is angry, part of me is sad, part of me wants to laugh and part of me is frightened. I don't want to think about my father, about the times I've been into his library when he's been working, when all along the closed-off shelves were full of lemons. I don't want to wonder what's inside his head, because what kind of crazy must it be?

As for the books . . . thinking of them gives me a pain inside so sharp that I can't breathe. How could he throw away Mum's books? How could he even bring himself to do that? Does he feel *nothing*?

Mae's parents are very kind. Her dad takes Christopher upstairs to race cars or trains or something, and Mae's mum gets me a hot chocolate and suggests we sit on the sofa and watch a film. Mae wants to watch *Frozen*, and I've never seen it, so she puts on the DVD and we sink into the sofa. The hot chocolate is warming and slips down easily, and the film is good, but I'm so exhausted I fall asleep before we're even halfway through.

In the morning I wake in a soft bed in the spare room, with a duvet over me. It has a pattern of little blue flowers. There is a white chest of drawers with round knobs for handles, and a pale blue carpet and a pine wardrobe in the corner. The lamp by my bed has a white shade with green leaves on it. I've only been in here once, when Mae was looking for a spare sheet in the bottom of the wardrobe. Outside, it's still raining. I can hear the pattering on the window.

The door is pushed open, and it's Mae, wearing yellow pyjamas.

'Hello,' she says. 'Did you sleep well?'

'Fine, thank you. It's still raining then?'

'Yes, the forecast says it'll rain all day.'

We are like old people having a conversation.

We get dressed for school. I feel as though I'm in two parts. Half of me feels quite usual – happy, even, at the fact that I've had a sleepover at Mae's house. The other half is shouting at me from behind a glass wall, silent. That's the half that's reminding me about yesterday, but I don't want to hear it. I want to pretend it didn't happen.

Just before lunchtime, Miss Spotlin calls me over. 'Calypso,' she says, 'you and I are going to go to Mrs Gilkes's office as soon as the bell goes, all right? There are some people who want to talk to you.'

'What people?'

Miss Spotlin puts her hand on my arm and looks at me in a friendly way. 'Don't worry. It's nothing bad. I'm coming with you.'

'What about my lunch?'

'The canteen staff will put something aside for you.'

We go to the head's office and knock on the door. Mrs Gilkes opens it and says, 'Hello, Calypso. Come on in.'

I am glad Miss Spotlin is with me because my tummy feels very fluttery. In Mrs Gilkes's office are two women. The first woman is tall with fluffy hair that's half brown, half white. She has glasses with funky designs on the arms, and she smiles at me. The second woman is shorter and very plump. She has a pale face with many lines around her eyes. She smiles too, but there's something in her gaze that makes me feel as though she's trying to see inside me.

Mrs Gilkes has arranged some chairs for us, so we sit in an awkward circle.

'Now,' says Mrs Gilkes, 'these ladies are from social services, Calypso. Something happened yesterday at home, is that right?'

I nod.

'They've come to make sure you're all right and to see if there's anything they can do to help.'

I feel even more nervous at this. What if they don't think I'm all right? What would they do? Would they take me away? Maybe I'm not all right. Maybe I need a hospital or something, to fix the strange feelings inside me.

'My name is Antonia,' says the tall woman with the funky glasses, 'and this is my colleague, Sarah. Please don't worry, Calypso. We don't want to interfere, but we think we might be able to help you and your father get through a difficult time.' She pauses for a moment. 'Shall I tell you a bit about what we do?'

She tells me about another family they helped recently where the father died in a car crash and the mother got so depressed she couldn't look after her three children. Antonia arranged for the mother to talk to a doctor and she slowly got better, and the three kids went on a special day trip to a theme park.

I'm a bit confused. Do they want to send me to a theme park? Because I don't really like rides.

Antonia says, 'But of course every family is different, and we can help in lots of different ways. Do you think your family might need some help?'

I lick my lips. The word 'family' doesn't seem quite right to me. 'There's only me and my dad.'

Antonia nods. 'You haven't got any uncles or aunts or grandparents?'

'Yes, some grandparents,' I say, 'but they live in Australia. I haven't seen them for years.'

The other lady, Sarah, puts her head on one side. Her eyes are very blue. 'I hear you like books, Calypso,' she says.

I am surprised. 'Yes.'

'Have you read *Matilda*?' she asks. 'It's my favourite book.'

I am even more surprised that a grown-up's favourite book is one written for children. 'Yes,' I say. 'I really liked it too. But *George's Marvellous Medicine* is funnier.'

She laughs. 'Yes. And *The Twits*.'

I smile. 'That's good too.'

'What are you reading at the moment?'

'*Holes*,' I tell her. 'I borrowed it from Mae. It's really good. We swap books. She lent me *The Diary of a Young Girl* too.'

All the other people in the room go, 'Ohh.'

'A fantastic book,' says Sarah, nodding. 'What did you think of it?'

'I liked it,' I say. 'I thought it was very sad. But it didn't make me cry, not like Mae. She cries at everything.'

Sarah glances briefly at Miss Spotlin, who says, 'Mae is Calypso's best friend.'

'Ah,' says Sarah. 'Good.'

Antonia pushes her glasses a bit further up her nose. 'Calypso,' she says, 'we wonder if you could tell us what happened yesterday?'

20

'What did you say?' asks Mae a bit later. We are sitting in the canteen, just the two of us. Everyone else has gone to class, but because I missed lunch break, I'm allowed to sit here with Mae for half an hour and eat the food they saved for me.

I shrug. 'Just what happened. I think. It's a bit fuzzy in my head, you know?'

Mae nods. 'What are they going to do?'

'Talk to my dad.' My stomach feels funny about this. 'They said they were going straight to my house to see him. They spoke to him on the phone before they came here.' In my pocket, I finger a little square of card. Antonia's business card, with her phone number on it. 'Ring if you need me,' she said kindly. How will I know if I need her? And what can she do anyway?

I'm not sure I want to go home. I wonder if I

could just go and stay with Mae for a bit longer. But what would Dad do without me?

'Do they think . . .' Mae hesitates. 'Do they think there's something wrong with him?'

'I don't know.'

She leaves it at that.

21

When I get home, Dad isn't in his library. He's in the sitting room, which is strange, because we hardly ever use that room. It's at the front of the house, on the right as you go in through the front door, with a big bay window that matches the one on the other side of the front door – the library window. There's a tree outside this window too. Even when it's bare in winter it shadows the house. Our house has a lot of shadows, it seems.

Mae's mum has come in with me. She offered, and I didn't have the courage to refuse. There's a sofa with a green William Morris pattern on it, and a matching armchair, with some big green and white squashy cushions. The curtains are pale green and the walls are cream with a patterned wallpaper. A clock they call a 'carriage clock' ticks quietly on the mantelpiece, and two landscape paintings of the Lake District hang either side. The room is dusty, and even though there's a television, we hardly ever watch it. It's on right now, though, showing some children's drama programme about werewolves. The volume is turned down very low, so the voices sound like they're whispering in the silence.

Mum liked this room. She used to sit in here in the evenings after I'd gone to bed, sketching or reading. Reading the books that used to be behind the shutters in the library.

Sometimes Dad would sit and read in here too, both of them focused intently on their own work. The only sounds would be their regular breathing and the turning of a page. I can remember being told to go and play somewhere else, because my bricks and toy cars and dolls were 'too noisy'. And then Mum would look at me, and her face would soften, and she would come with me and we'd play trains in the kitchen or do painting in the garden.

She was always better at make-believe than Dad. She would have been so excited about Mae's Wendy house. She'd have painted murals on the walls and sat inside with us and made up silly poems and giggled. It feels like when she died most of the fun and the craziness went out of our lives. Or the nice kind of craziness did anyway. Now it appears Dad has a crazy all his own.

Dad is standing by the sofa, one hand resting on the back of it, as though he needs its support. He looks very tired.

'Calypso,' he says.

'Hi, Dad.' My tongue feels heavy in my mouth.

He looks at Mae's mum.

'I won't stay,' she says. 'Calypso wanted me to come in with her.'

'It's all right,' he tells her. Then he says to me, 'I thought we might watch some television.'

'Oh. All right.'

He sits down in the armchair, and after a moment's pause I put my bag down on the floor and take off my coat.

'I suppose . . .' I say to Mae's mum.

She smiles at me in a reassuring way. 'You'll be fine. And you've got my number, so ring if you need anything.'

Then she goes.

I sit down on the sofa. Dad turns up the volume and we both stare at the TV. Two characters are having an argument about who can be trusted. Then there's a family scene, where the father interferes with what the kids want to do.

Dad says, 'Why doesn't he want them to go outside?'

'I don't know,' I say. 'I haven't seen it before.'

We watch a bit more. Some of the characters turn into wolves. I can almost feel Dad's eyebrows climbing up his forehead.

'Well,' he says as the episode ends, 'that was . . . educational.' Then he mutes the volume and says, 'Calypso, we need to talk.'

I say nothing. I find it hard to look at him.

'Some people from social services came to see me today. I gather they went to see you too.'

'Yes, at school.'

'What did you think?'

I am puzzled. 'What do you mean?'

'Did you think they were helpful?'

'Uh . . . I guess.' I feel as though this isn't a good answer. The TV screen flickers with a trailer for some other programme. 'They were nice,' I add lamely.

He nods. 'They want me to go for counselling.'

'Counselling?'

'They think . . . I need to talk to someone. About your mother.' He swallows.

I can't say anything. Is that why he's in this room – her room? To think about her? Is he sorry he threw out her books?

He goes on, 'I think maybe they're right. I have been – internalising. For protection, you know?'

I don't really. 'Er . . .'

'Maybe it's about time I talked to someone.'

My throat tightens with tears. Why couldn't he talk to *me*? How did everything get this bad?

'There'll be another meeting soon,' he says. 'All of us in a room together, to talk through the plan.'

'I know. They told me.'

He leans towards me, resting his elbows on his knees. 'Calypso, I'm very sorry. About the books – well, about everything. I've been . . . selfish. I haven't been looking after you very well.'

My hands are tightly clasped in my lap. I should be grateful that he's talking like this. His words should be reassuring, but I feel frightened. Dad doesn't say these kinds of things. And he doesn't use this tone of voice – the tone that says he's vulnerable, that he's unsure of himself. What's more, we're here, in the sitting room, in *Mum's* room, and that feels wrong too.

I feel like I'm standing on the edge of a cliff, and I can't stop myself falling off.

I wish I hadn't discovered the lemons.

22

Mae sees beneath my calm exterior. 'Are you okay?' she asks.

'I'm fine.'

'No, you're not.'

'Well, if you knew I wasn't, why did you ask?' I snap.

She gives a little sigh. 'We're kindred spirits, Calypso, I know you. You can tell me everything that's in your heart.'

I brush at my eyes. We are in class, creating bar charts. I have drawn my chart already and only need to colour it in.

'Things are changing,' I say. 'I don't like change.'

'Bad changing?' asks Mae, concentrating on her own chart.

'I don't know! Maybe.'

'Everything changes,' says Mae. 'Mum says it's

not good for things to stay the same for too long.'

'Why not?'

She hesitates. 'I don't know exactly. But it's good that things have come out, isn't it?'

'Is it? I don't know what to expect now. Will Dad be different? Am *I* supposed to be different?'

Mae smiles at me. 'Don't be different. I wouldn't like it!'

Her words are comforting, but then I remember something Antonia mentioned. 'They want me to go to a young carers' group.'

'What's that?'

'It's a group for kids who look after their parents.'

Mae frowns slightly. 'Look after them how?'

'Well – I'm not sure. Doing the cooking. Washing-up. Making sure their parents eat or get dressed, stuff like that.'

She stares at me properly. 'Do you have to do that for your dad?'

I hesitate. 'I mostly make my own supper,' I admit in a low voice. 'Dad doesn't remember to eat because he's so busy working.' Doubt grips me. Has he actually been working? Has it all been a pretence? 'And I put the laundry on, and hang up the clothes. And I make him cups of tea. But I don't have to get him dressed or anything. I mean, he's not *ill*. Not – not in a normal way, anyway.'

She seems unsure of what to say next. 'You never said. Isn't it hard, doing all that? I don't even know how to cook.'

'Neither do I, really,' I say. 'I mostly heat things up in the oven or the microwave. Though I can do things with eggs – scrambled, boiled, you know. And you can use up lots of things in an omelette.'

'Wow.' Mae picks up a blue pencil and starts colouring in her bar chart. 'So you'll go to meet other kids who do those things too. That might be interesting.'

'Mmm,' I say. I'm a bit nervous of meeting new people. But how can I tell them I don't want to go?

'What about the books?' Mae asks.

I know which ones she means. Mum's books from the library, the ones Dad removed from the shelves and replaced with lemons. *They're behind the shed*, he'd said.

I haven't dared look yet. I can't. Something about the thought of them there hurts me too much. It's crazy, because the longer they stay out there, the more damaged they'll be. But they've been out there for months already, haven't they? The state some of those lemons were in . . . it would have taken over six months for them to get like that. Maybe a year.

I'm not sure I'm strong enough to face up to that just yet.

I shrug. 'I'll do something about them soon.'

Mae bites her lip but says nothing.

23

Dad is doing more things around the house. I come home one day to find he's hoovered the bedrooms. I can't remember the last time he did that. And there's food in the fridge. It's not food that's very good for you – there are a lot of ready meals – but at least I don't have to wonder what I'm going to eat every day.

He seems a bit lost, though. He drifts from room to room, moving things from one place to another and then back again. Now that he's finished his book, he doesn't know what to do with himself. He switched on his computer the other day and I saw there were three new emails from a publisher, offering him some work on new manuscripts. But he just sighed when he saw them and switched the computer off without replying.

When I get home from school, we go to the

kitchen together, where he makes me a mug of tea and asks me how school was.

'Fine,' I say, and then we sit in an awkward silence for a while.

'So,' I say, 'what have you done today?'

He draws a breath, as though it's an effort. 'I cleaned the bathroom,' he says. 'But we'd run out of bleach, so I went to the shop. I wasn't sure what scent to get. I hope you like lavender.'

I shrug. 'It's all right.'

He says, 'Well, it was that or . . . lemon.'

I bite my lip, staring at my mug of tea and deliberately burning my palms on it.

'Sorry,' he says. 'I didn't mean to say that word. Er . . . then I came home, and I tried to make some soup. I found a nice recipe for potato and leek. But I forgot that our blender doesn't work.'

This is all wrong. He doesn't sound like himself.

'Were you warm enough?' he asks me. 'Because it's been cold out today, and I thought maybe you'd forgotten your gloves.'

Since when did my father talk about the weather? Who is this person? I don't know how to talk to him.

I get up abruptly, slopping my tea slightly. 'I've got homework to do,' I say. 'I'd better get on with it.'

'Oh.' His face falls in disappointment for a moment, before he forces a smile. 'All right. Chicken and chips for dinner?'

'Fine.'

I go to my room and stare at the walls. Will I get home one day to discover my house has turned into a regular three-bed, with a proper garden and a dog? Because the person downstairs is a complete stranger, so it wouldn't surprise me if everything else changed as well.

If things change, will I change too?

If my father is no longer the same person, who am I?

24

The young carers' group is held in the local family centre and the heating is on full blast. I am pleased. It's the second week of November, the evenings are getting colder and I hate being cold. I hesitate in the doorway. Dad dropped me off, but I didn't want him to come in. He keeps offering to do things with me, but I know it's because he's making an effort and that makes me not really believe he wants to, so I feel cross – and that makes me say no when he offers. I know it's unreasonable of me, but I can't help it.

There are two adults in the room – a man and a woman – and three kids. There's a table set out with painting things on it, and in that moment I decide to turn and run. I don't want to paint. Mum painted.

But it's too late. The woman has seen me. 'Hello!'

she says cheerfully, and heads over. 'Are you Calypso?'

I nod.

She smiles. She's younger than I expected, and she has long brown hair tied back in a plait. 'I'm Abby. Come and join us.'

I smile back, and she walks me into the room.

'This is Raj.'

The man grins at me. He looks a bit older than Abby, but not by much.

'Hi, Calypso. This probably feels kind of freaky to you at the moment. Don't worry. Just go with the flow, okay?'

I nod, wondering what on earth that means. Go with what flow? What will we be doing?

'Not everyone is here yet,' Abby tells me. 'We should have another three any minute.' She introduces me to the three kids who are already there. Lisiella and Krystal are girls, a bit younger than me I think. They look like they've known each other for a long time, since one of them is doing the other's hair. They smile at me in between excited discussions about a pop band I've never heard of. The third is a boy, Reece, leaning against the window, thumbs flying over his mobile phone. He doesn't even look up.

'Everyone who comes to the group is a carer,' Abby tells me. 'When they're at home, they have to do adult things, like cooking and cleaning and making sure their mum or dad takes medication. Here they can switch all that off and be kids for an hour.'

'Oh,' I say, like I understand, but I'm not sure I do. Do I have to switch part of myself off? How do I do that?

Raj glances at the clock on the wall. 'We could get started,' he says, and Abby nods.

'Might as well. The others will come when they can.'

I feel a bit surprised. They don't seem cross that the other three kids are late. At school it would matter.

We sit down at the big table, and Abby explains what we're going to do. 'We've got some wooden photo frames,' she says, holding one up. 'And lots of different colours of paint. So you can do whatever design you like – either for yourself, or as a present for someone else. Maybe think about if one of your friends or relatives has a birthday coming up.'

Lisiella and Krystal make excited squeaking

noises and immediately reach for brushes and paints. Reece is still looking at his phone.

'Put that away now, mate,' Raj tells him gently.

For a moment I think that Reece is going to ignore him, since he doesn't show any sign that he's heard. But then he puts his phone in his pocket and stares at the table.

'I'm no good at painting,' he says gruffly.

'Everyone can paint,' Abby says. 'You can paint the whole frame blue if you like. It doesn't have to have patterns on it.' She smiles at me. 'Got an idea of what you want to do?'

'Er . . .' I say. I'm not sure that 'walk out of the door' is one of the options.

A girl with the longest plait I've ever seen comes running in. 'Sorry! Mum dropped all her tablets on the floor and I had to find them before the cat ate them.'

Lisiella and Krystal giggle, and the girl glares at them.

'It's not funny! The last time the cat ate one of her tablets, she had to have her stomach pumped at the vet and it cost ninety quid!'

Lisiella and Krystal immediately sober up.

'Ooh,' says Lisiella. 'That's *criminal*.'

'That's why my dad says we can't have any pets,' says Krystal. 'They cost way too much.'

'Come and sit down,' says Abby, 'and meet Calypso. Calypso, this is Lina.'

Lina says hi to me and then sits down at the table. 'What are we doing?'

Over the next twenty minutes, I paint my photo frame. Two more boys join us – Tyler, and someone whose name I don't catch. They do a lot of play-fighting and tip over two of the paint pots, which annoys Krystal. 'Now I'll have to wash this!' she exclaims, staring at her skirt, which has a big red splodge on it. 'And it won't be dry by tomorrow! You idiots!' They apologise, and Abby promises to help Krystal remove the paint once it's dried.

I choose yellow for my frame, and paint the whole thing the same colour, filling in any imperfections in the wood with extra dabs of paint. There's glitter too, and I sprinkle gold over the yellow as evenly as I can.

'That looks lovely,' says Abby. 'Like sunshine or happiness.'

I freeze. *Happiness* – my mother's painting, the one that was in the exhibition at the National Gallery. The picture that's all yellow with glitter sprinkles on it. I feel cold all over. I didn't even realise that's what I was doing.

'I love painting, don't you?' asks Lisiella cheerfully.

I realise she's talking to me. 'Er,' I say. 'It's all right. I prefer reading.'

Lisiella looks sceptical. 'Reading?' she echoes. 'You *like* it?'

'Yes. Why, don't you?'

She shakes her head. 'What's it for?'

I am nonplussed. No one has ever asked me this question before. What is reading *for*?

Abby is looking at me. I wonder if she knows how to answer, but she doesn't say anything. Instead she gives me an encouraging smile.

I say to Lisiella, 'Reading is for everything. You can go places you can't in real life. You can be people you're not. You can do things you wouldn't be allowed to do.'

Lisiella stares very hard at her picture frame. 'I don't need reading for any of that stuff,' she says. 'I go round to my friend's house and play on her DS.'

'Oh,' I say. 'I've never done that.'

'You've never played on a DS?' says Lisiella. She sounds disbelieving.

'No.'

'What about an Xbox?'

'No.'

'A Wii?'

I feel a bit nervous. I'm not really sure what one of those is. It sounds like a made-up name. Is she testing me? Will she laugh if I say the wrong thing? 'I haven't played any video-game . . . things,' I say.

Now everyone else around the table is looking at me, amazed.

'You're joking,' says Reece.

'You must have played *something*,' says Krystal. 'Everyone's played *something*.'

'I've played games on computer,' I say desperately. I have, but only the ones at school that are educational.

The others shake their heads.

'They're rubbish,' declares Reece. 'You should play *Grand Theft Auto*.'

Attention immediately switches. Krystal demands to know when she can come round to his house and have a go, and Lisiella shouts that no one should be playing it because it's too violent and anyway he's too young. Lina says she's heard that video games make people violent and Reece snorts and says he's never killed anyone so she's talking rubbish.

I look down at my hands, seeing dabs of yellow paint on my fingers, and feel hot and cold. Am I really so different from everyone else, even here? Christopher has a tablet thing that he plays games on, but Mae and I are always too busy writing our stories or reading books. Have I missed out on something absolutely vital to my life?

Raj clears his throat. 'I think that's enough of that,' he says. 'Time to chat.'

The others, still arguing over video games, get up and bring their chairs into a space on the other side of the room, forming a circle. I do the same, unsure.

'Don't be alarmed,' Abby tells me. 'We always have a bit of circle time. It helps to share our worries and our problems with people who understand.' She sees my face. 'You don't have to say anything if you don't want to.'

I breathe out in relief.

Lina goes first. 'I took Mum back to see the consultant yesterday. He wants to try her on these new drugs, which might help with her muscle spasms. They've got worse since the last relapse. She keeps knocking stuff over, and dropping things because she can't grip them properly. I keep having to clear up after her.' She heaves a big sigh. 'But hopefully the new drugs will help, as long as she keeps taking them. She's going through another phase of not wanting to take anything because she says the pills make her depressed.'

I am listening very quietly and intently. It sounds like Lina's mum is really sick. My dad doesn't have anything like that. Muscle spasms? Are they like cramp?

'Lina's mum has multiple sclerosis,' Abby says to me, and I jump, startled.

'Oh,' I say. I don't know what that is.

'Do you need more help?' Raj asks Lina. 'Should I speak to Antonia?'

Lina has the same social worker as me! I don't quite know why I'm surprised. I suppose they have lots of children to look after.

Lina shrugs. 'Like what? She's always so busy.'

Raj says, 'She does her best.'

'Yeah, I know. Too much work, that's what my mum says. They've all got too much work. That's why she's never in the office.' Lina pulls a face. 'Got to make the best of it, don't we?'

Krystal tells us that her mum managed to go to a job interview by herself, which doesn't sound all that amazing to me until I realise that her mum is blind. And then Tyler tells us about his little brother passing his swimming certificate and how he's really proud of him. Tyler's dad has something called post-traumatic stress disorder after being in the army and his mum has depression. It sounds like there's a lot of arguing in their house, and Tyler has three younger brothers that he looks after, getting them dressed and ready for school in the morning and everything. He's the same age as me and worried about what will happen when he goes to secondary school, because he'll have to catch a bus that leaves earlier than his brothers have to leave for their school.

Lisiella complains that her dad won't let her have a mobile phone. Reece says nothing.

'Calypso, did you want to tell us a bit about yourself?' Abby asks me kindly.

But I can't. How can I? What problems do I have compared with the others? And how can I possibly tell them that my dad has been keeping lemons on bookshelves? How would people who play Xboxes and don't read books react to that extreme weirdness?

I shrink back in my chair and shake my head.

The others look a bit disappointed, except Reece, who has pulled his phone out of his pocket again.

Abby and Raj get out some games, and I play Snap with Lisiella, Krystal and Lina until it's time to go home.

'See you next week,' Abby and Raj say as I head out to find Dad's car.

I smile and wave at them. It's been a weird evening. Everyone there looks after their parents, and sometimes their brothers and sisters. It's the wrong way round, really. The parents should be doing the looking-after. It's like the children have to be the grown-ups.

Is that what I've been doing for Dad? Has our family life been the wrong way round ever since Mum died?

25

I go to my library that evening and sit on the floor, staring at the books from my mother's childhood. I pull out an old copy of *Anne of Green Gables* and see her name in careful joined-up handwriting on the first page: *Coral Costello, aged 9 ¼*. I run my finger over it. I'm sure she must have loved Anne too – her wildness, her spirit, her imagination. Did she dream of one day sharing this story with me? How did she feel when she knew – when she was told – that she would never see me grow up? I rest my hand over her writing and close my eyes.

The air stills. This room is my sanctuary. I sit and breathe in the invisible stories all around me, the characters trapped between the pages of the books only until someone reads the words, and then they're set free. Books can take you places and show you people you'd never meet in real life.

I breathe in the faint scent of oil paint too – and suddenly I can see Mum in my mind's eye, clear as day, her red hair shining in the sunlight (it's sunny again!) and a big smile on her face. A great sense of warmth rushes through me. She's *here*; I haven't forgotten her, and I won't, ever.

It's time to rescue the books from the library of lemons.

I go downstairs and tell Dad, 'We need to get those books from behind the shed.'

He is sitting at his desk, staring at nothing. His eyes close. 'I'm tired, Calypso.'

'So am I. But we need to get the books.'

'It's dark.'

'Now, Dad. It's important.'

He heaves the biggest sigh ever, deflating, like all the breath is leaving his body.

I wait, impatiently. 'Come on.'

Eventually he says, 'All right.'

It takes him ages to put on his boots by the back door. My boots are too small and pinch my toes, but I hardly notice because I am shifting from one foot to the other, feeling irritation grow by the second. Why is he so slow?

We take a torch into the garden. The shed is at

the end, with a small gap between the back of it and the hedge. Dad shines the torch into the gap. I swallow. There are nine or ten cardboard boxes of books, stacked on top of each other. How did he even fit them into this gap?

'We must bring them inside,' I say.

Dad opens his mouth and then closes it again. He hands me the torch and reaches for the nearest box. It takes a lot of pulling and wriggling to get it to move, and then one side falls away completely, spilling paperbacks onto the grass. I see *Pride and Prejudice*, *The Handmaid's Tale*, *Enduring Love* – Mum's books.

'Pick them up!' I say, reaching desperately to grab as many as I can. We fill our arms and carry them back to the kitchen where I stack them on the table.

They are in a pitiful state. Some are black and mouldy round the edges; others have come apart at the binding. All are damp.

I am filled with fire. We must save them. It is my mission. 'We have to get them all in. Not just Mum's – all of them.'

Dad balks at this. 'We can't get them all tonight, Calypso. It's dark and cold, and we have nowhere to put them.'

'Yes we do,' I say obstinately. 'We have your library.'

After all, the shelves are no longer occupied by lemons.

Dad is cold and damp himself by the time he's brought all the books inside. It takes him nearly two hours. Every now and then he mutters in a complaining way, but then he glances at me and stops.

Some of the books are beyond saving. The enormous atlas disintegrates in my hands, the seams dissolved and the paper blotched and unreadable. But others have survived better. I spread them all out over the shelves and the floor of the library, pages open to the air to dry. There are so many that by the time we have finished there is no space to place even one foot inside the room. We stand and stare from the doorway at the metres and metres of words. My back aches and I should have been in bed hours ago, but I feel satisfaction at the sight. I can almost see Mum nodding and smiling at me.

Behind me, Dad gives a big sigh. I can't tell if it's a sigh of happiness or a sigh of sadness. Does he miss his lemons? I daren't ask.

'Thank you,' I say instead.

26

That night, I dream about books. I am in a forest, where books are literally growing on trees, and I am hungry. It's dark, and chilly, and my stomach growls, and so I reach up to a branch and pluck down a book. It is a blue hardback. I take a bite, and the book melts between my teeth into something like a marshmallow sandwich. I pluck a red paperback from another branch, and it is crisp and crunchy like an apple. I eat and eat and eat until the branches are bare and my stomach is full. And then I sit down on the grass and groan, because now I feel sick.

And my father appears in between the trees, saying, 'Calypso, you know perfectly well that you need a pencil and a trained ferret to find your way through the woods. Have I taught you nothing?'

Then he turns into a lemon and rolls away through the trees, and I can hear my mother singing, which is strange, because I don't think she sang much when I was little, but in the dream I'm sure it's her. And the singing makes me breathe out all the books I've eaten in a long sigh. All these words come spilling and tumbling out of my mouth and lie about me on the forest floor. And I lie down too, my hair and fingers and feet tangling in words and letters and sentences, and the sunlight comes dancing through the trees, and I feel happy.

27

'So are all the books there?' asks Mae when I tell her about our rescue mission. 'In the library?'

'Yes. They need to dry out. Some of them might be all right – not as good as they were, but good enough to read and put back on the shelves. I think the others will have to be thrown away.'

She nods with a grimace. We are round at her house after school. Mae's expanding one of the intricate patterns on her wall and I am colouring in some pictures in a colouring book. Dad is at a counselling session.

'I'm glad some of them will be okay,' she says. 'What about your mum's books? Have you saved all of them?'

'No.' I look down at my picture. 'I mean, yes, I've brought them all in. But the pages of *To Kill a Mockingbird* are all stuck together and I think even when it's dried out it'll be no good.'

'You could buy a new copy,' Mae says.

'It wouldn't be hers,' I say. There is a pause, and a fierceness sweeps through me. 'How could he *do* it, Mae? I mean, getting rid of your own books is one thing, but how could he do that to hers? She's *dead*! They were *her* things. They were meant for *me*. Did he *know* how spiteful it would be to chuck them in the garden? Did he *want* to hurt me? Or is he so completely loopy that he didn't even think about it?'

'I don't know,' Mae says in a hesitant voice. 'I guess when things aren't . . . normal, then . . .' She trails off.

'Am *I* normal?' I say bluntly.

She looks startled, a red felt-tip poised in mid-air. 'Well, you seem normal to me.'

'Have you got a dictionary?'

She sticks out an arm and pulls a thick book off a nearby shelf. It takes us a while to find the right page.

'Normal,' she says. 'Conforming to the standard or common type. Usual, regular, natural.'

'So then something that is common is normal,'

I say. 'So if most people have blue eyes, then brown eyes are not normal.'

'Brown eyes are common too,' objects Mae. 'It doesn't say you can only have one type of normal.'

'Good point. So if lots of kids live with just one parent, that's common enough to be normal, right?'

'I guess so.'

'And lots of people die from cancer, don't they? So that makes that normal too.'

Mae frowns. 'Dying from a disease when you're not old shouldn't be normal.'

'But *shouldn't* isn't the same as *is*,' I say, shaking my head. 'Wanting things to be different doesn't make them that.' I feel compelled to go on. 'But lots of people don't die from cancer either, which is *also* normal. So . . . how can two opposite things both be normal?'

Mae bites her lip thoughtfully. 'It sort of makes you wonder how anyone works out what *normal* is.'

'And if no one is really sure . . .' I say. 'If people are just making up their own idea of *normal*, then . . .'

'Then anything is normal. And everything,' concludes Mae.

There is silence in the room. Mae and I stare at each other.

There are fireworks in my brain. Ever since Mum died, I've felt not normal. Like I didn't fit in. I preferred reading books to making friends. I lived with a dad who didn't seem to notice I was there half the time, and who didn't like hugging, and who insisted on inner strength. I didn't *mind*, exactly – but I didn't feel *normal.*

But what if normal isn't really a thing?

What if I'm normal in a world where *everything and nothing* is normal? The thought is incredible.

And then Mae adds, looking down at the page, 'It says "psychology" too. In terms of "normal". Er. Approximately average in any psychological trait, such as intelligence, personality or emotional adjustment. Also, free from any mental disorder, sane.' She closes the book.

'But,' I say, carrying through my previous thought, 'what does that even mean, if anything can be normal?' I look at her. 'Do you think maybe throwing out my mum's books seemed normal to my dad?'

'I suppose it must have. Because he needed the shelves. For his . . . um . . . lemons.'

The way she says it makes me want to laugh. It's the silliest thing ever!

Mae casts a glance at me, and I see that the corner of her mouth has twitched up a bit. She says, 'At least it wasn't, I dunno, fingers or something.'

'Fingers?'

'You know, like a serial killer. Or dead babies.'

My mouth drops open in horror. 'Mae! That's just . . . *eww*! How can you think up such horrible things?'

Her eyes are mischievous. 'What? I'm just saying, it could be worse. I mean – *lemons*. Not exactly the stuff of nightmares.'

I can't help a grin. 'That's what you think. I dream about them now. They freak me out. Dad actually *turned into* a lemon in last night's dream, and rolled away through a forest.'

She laughs. 'What I mean is, even if your dad's a bit mad, it's not like he's dangerous or something, is it? Keeping lemons on shelves is freaky, but it's not run-for-the-hills, is it?'

'I suppose not.'

'How's his counselling going?'

I shrug. 'All right, I think. Sometimes he seems

upset when he comes home. I think they make him talk about my mum.'

'Oh.' Mae goes quiet for a moment. Then she says, 'I guess he must miss her a lot.'

'I guess so . . .' I say slowly, feeling puzzled. 'He's never *said* he does. He always says you should use inner strength to cope with sad feelings.'

Mae glances at me, her eyebrows pulled together as though she doesn't understand. 'What do you mean?'

'Inner strength is the thing you have to depend on,' I say, going back to my colouring. 'When you're sad or worried or lonely or something, you have to look inside yourself to find your inner strength. And you use it to wipe away the bad feelings and make yourself happy again. That's what makes you strong, you see.'

Mae still looks baffled. 'Wow. I don't think I've ever looked for my inner strength. Do you think I have any?'

'Everyone does,' I say, nodding.

'Do you think . . .' Mae hesitates. 'Do you think your dad's inner strength ran out, or something?'

I stare at my picture. 'Maybe there's a limit,' I say, thinking out loud. 'Maybe, if you lock away the sadness for too long, it all builds up. Like filling a tank. And one day the tank bursts and you have way more sadness than normal because it's all been stored away.'

Mae nods. 'And it wouldn't matter how much inner strength you have.'

'Maybe it's important to let yourself be sad sometimes,' I say. 'To stop the tank filling up.'

There's a small blotch on my picture where the blue and the yellow have run together. I dab at it with my sleeve. 'It was very quick, her illness, you know. She had hardly any time to do what she wanted before she died. I sometimes think, if they hadn't found the cancer and told her, would she still be alive? I mean, did telling her make it happen?'

'Are you okay?' asks Mae.

'I'm fine.'

'It's just that you're crying.'

'Am I?'

She moves my picture out of the way gently. 'You must miss her a lot.'

Maybe I have a tank of sadness in me too.

Mae shuffles over and puts her arm around me. 'It's okay to cry,' she says in a voice that sounds like a nurse. 'It's nothing to do with inner strength. You haven't got a mum. It's a good thing to cry about.'

So I do. And Mae gives me a proper hug while I do it.

28

Dad comes to pick me up and stays for dinner at Mae's house. We have chicken wings with sticky sauce and rice and peas. It's delicious. Dad looks a bit disappointed that there isn't enough for seconds.

Mae's mum notices. 'Do you cook at home?' she asks him.

'A bit,' he says. Then he pauses and adds, 'I should do more. But I get very tired.'

'This is an easy recipe,' Mae's mum says. 'Ten minutes of chopping things, and then you just put it in the oven. And cook the rice.'

Dad looks down at his empty plate. For a moment I think he's going to say something else, but he doesn't.

'I'll have the recipe,' I say. 'I like cooking.'

Dad gets up abruptly and leaves the room.

We all stare at each other. I feel my cheeks get

hot, and my eyes fill with tears. I *do* like cooking! I've cooked for Dad loads of times! Is he angry with me? Why?

No one is quite sure what to do.

'Are you okay?' Mae whispers to me.

I nod fiercely, not looking at her.

Mae's dad starts talking about something that happened to him on the way to work last week. Mae's mum listens and asks questions and laughs in the right place, collecting the plates and bringing a fruit salad to the table for pudding. Christopher complains that he doesn't like fruit and starts picking his nose. Mae keeps sneaking sideways looks at me and although I know it's because she's worried about me, I wish she wouldn't. It makes me embarrassed. I accept a bowl of fruit salad and stare at it.

When Dad comes back in, he says, 'Sorry, everyone,' and sits down at the table. But he doesn't explain why he left the room, and he won't catch my eye, so I wonder if he's still angry with me for some reason. My throat feels too tight to eat.

There's another awkward pause, and then Mae's mum says, 'Are you looking forward to Christmas, Calypso?'

I'm not, really. It's just going to be Dad and me,

like it always is, and I've never minded before. But this year the thought of just him and me, sitting in a cold house, reading books . . . it frightens me. It's lonely, and sad, and Christmas should be about family . . . and we haven't got any. Mum's parents are dead, and Dad's parents emigrated to Australia just after I was born, so I think I've only met them twice. And I have no aunts or uncles or cousins – not a single one. Can a family be just two people? Is that *normal*?

'I . . .' I begin, but then I don't know what to add to the sentence. So I bite on my lip instead and poke at my fruit salad.

'Can she come here?' Mae asks suddenly.

'What?'

Everyone looks at Mae.

'*They*,' says Mae carefully. 'Can *they* come here? Calypso and her dad?'

My eyes dry magically, as though blown by a fairy wind. Christmas at Mae's house! It is an overwhelming thought. I can't allow myself to think of it too much. Surely . . .

I turn to my father. He looks like a hamster does when you reach in to pick it up. Not sure which way to run.

'Er . . .' he says. 'Well . . .'

'Oh, please,' I say, my mouth forming the words without any air.

'Well,' says Mae's dad, 'let's see how things go, shall we?'

After dinner, I go to get my coat and Mae follows me to the hall. 'You *must* come for Christmas!' she whispers. 'It'd be *brilliant*! You *have* to persuade your dad!'

I grab her hands, my heart filled with fire. 'I will come if it takes every breath in my body.'

Mae squeezes my hands even more tightly. 'Come first thing in the morning and bring your stocking! We can open them together!'

I glance at Dad, but he's busy talking to Mae's dad. 'My stocking presents are never very good,' I whisper as quietly as I can.

Mae pulls me close and whispers into my ear, 'Then you can have some of mine.'

That settles it. I *have* to be at Mae's house for Christmas. I have to!

29

It's my fourth visit to the young carers' group and we're already into December. I still feel like the odd one out. Do Antonia and Sarah expect me to make friends with people just because they have parents who have problems? Is that enough for a friendship? I feel awkward because we don't seem to have anything else in common. It makes chatting hard. I tried to explain that on the phone to Antonia yesterday. She listened and then said kind things about it being early days. I wanted to ask if we were supposed to have another meeting – her and me and Sarah and Dad – but another phone rang in the background and she had to go.

Today at the group we're tearing pictures out of Christmas catalogues to make a huge collage to go on the wall. I find a spelling mistake on one of the pages and point it out to Lina. She seems amused, but Lisiella doesn't see what's wrong with the word.

'It says "buidling blocks", not "building blocks".' I show her.

She shrugs. 'Looks all right to me. But I'm dyslexic.'

I nod in sudden understanding. 'Is that why you don't like reading?'

'Yeah. It's too hard.'

I hesitate. 'Maybe you just haven't found the right sort of book.'

She shakes her head firmly. 'Nah. I've tried everything. My brain is stupid.'

I'm not sure what to say to this. Is her brain stupid? Maybe it is – is that a bad thing? 'There must be stuff you're good at. What do you like at school?'

'Hate school. Don't go much.' She smiles at me cheerfully.

'Oh,' I say, nonplussed. 'You mean, you – er – bunk off?'

'Yeah,' says Lisiella. 'It's better than being taught all that rubbish.' She doesn't actually say 'rubbish', she says a rude word. I'm trying to get used to the language here. The kids all use swear words easily, though I can't bring myself to do the same. The words feel odd in my mouth, like sour sweets.

'Doesn't your mum get cross if you don't go to school?' I ask.

Lisiella blows air out of her mouth in a disgusted way. 'Mum doesn't live with us any more. She's loopy.'

'She is?' I am suddenly interested. 'In what way?'

'She's got bipolar disorder.'

'What's that?'

'It's when you get really, really, *really* happy and do crazy things like spend all your money or drink a whole bottle of rum, or try to re-paint the house in the middle of the night. And then you get really, really sad and just sit in a corner and cry and want to kill yourself.'

I stare at her. 'Wow. That sounds – scary.'

Lisiella shrugs. 'Yeah. It is. It's why Dad split up with her. I wanted to live with Mum, but everyone said she wasn't fit to be left in charge of me and my brothers.'

She has two younger brothers – I know because she's told me before. They like to wrestle in the living room and are always knocking themselves out on the furniture or breaking their arms falling off the sofa. Lisiella says she knows all the nurses who work in Accident and Emergency because they've been there so often.

'So where does your mum live now?' I ask.

'In a B&B. I don't like it there, it smells. And Mum gets really depressed. But they've put her on some new medication and they say it should help.'

'Oh.' It sounds very different from my dad.

'Why are you here?' asks Lina, who has been quietly listening. 'What's wrong with your parents?'

I take a breath. I haven't told anyone about my life yet. 'My mum died,' I say. 'Cancer.'

'Oh.' Lina looks sympathetic. 'Bad luck.'

'What kind of cancer?' Lisiella wants to know.

'Ovarian,' I say.

She nods. 'That kind kills you fast, I think. My neighbour had it. They didn't find out until it was too late.'

I bite my lip. 'Yes. That's what happened to my mum too.'

'So you live with your dad?' asks Lina.

'Yes. It's just me and him. And I suppose . . . well, he's kind of loopy too. Only not like your mum, Lisiella. He's just a bit eccentric.'

She looks blank. 'What's that mean?'

'He's sort of forgetful. And a bit obsessive about weird things.'

'Like what?'

I tell them about the lemons. Part of me doesn't want to because it feels like I'm betraying Dad. But this is the place I'm supposed to talk about it, right?

Lisiella bursts out laughing. 'He filled the shelves with lemons? Ferr-rreaky!'

Lina says, 'Lisiella, don't be horrible,' but I can see her trying to hold back a smile.

'At least he isn't trying to kill himself,' I snap, and then catch my breath, horrified.

Lisiella's laugh stops abruptly and she looks down at the table. Her fingers clench into fists.

'I'm sorry,' I say quickly. 'I didn't mean to say that.'

'My mum sometimes says she would gas herself in her car if she could,' Lina says very quietly.

I feel awful. 'I'm so sorry. I shouldn't have said anything. But my dad . . . the lemon thing. It – it's scary. I mean, weird and kind of funny, but it was scary. Like there was all this stuff going on in his head that I never knew about.'

The other two nod and Lisiella gives a sigh.

'Brains are so weird. People are weird.'

'Is your dad getting help?' Lina asks me.

'Yes. Counselling.'

'Watch that,' Lisiella says in a warning tone.

'What do you mean?'

'They go funny in counselling. How long has he been going?'

'A couple of weeks?'

She nods. 'Look out. People get really depressed when they start going for therapy.'

'What? Why? I thought they were meant to get less depressed!'

'I dunno.' Lisiella shrugs. 'When my mum started going, she went off-the-wall loopy, even worse than usual. The therapist told us it was normal, that most people did this crashing thing to begin with, and then they started to get better.' She pulls a face. 'Still waiting for Mum to get better!'

I stare at the torn pieces of paper on the table. Is it true? Is Dad going to get even worse now he's getting help? What kind of crazy things could he do?

What would I do if he decides he wants to die?

30

Lisiella's words make me frightened, and I watch Dad very carefully for the next few days. But he just seems quiet and a bit sad, which is no different from usual. Normal, I guess. The fear stays, though, and I keep wondering if I'm going to come home from school one day and find him huddled in a corner, sobbing.

But instead when I get home one Tuesday I find him in the kitchen. The radio is on, playing something classical and stirring, and Dad is stirring too – rice in a pan on the stove. He turns to me and I feel slightly faint with surprise, because he looks happy. Actually happy, with a smile on his face and colour in his cheeks. The sight makes my jaw drop. And, for some reason, it makes me even more nervous.

'Isn't it a grim day out?' he says cheerfully. 'I

thought I'd make that chicken recipe to brighten things up.'

'Wow.' I put my bag down on the floor. It *is* a grim day out. I'm pretty wet from the constant drizzle and the drive-by splashing from the cars on the road. The bus was full of people, their breath steaming up the windows. The walk from the bus stop to my house was a cold one, and my coat is last year's and now too short at the wrists, so my hands are freezing. 'That sounds great. I need warming up.'

Dad says, 'Why don't you go and get changed? Put on some more layers. This'll be ready in about ten minutes.'

I don't say that it's an odd time to have supper – 3.45 p.m. – because when's the wrong time for supper if you're hungry? Instead, I go upstairs, throw my uniform on the floor and find the comfiest clothes I can, along with two pairs of socks and the slippers that are so worn out they're almost dangerous on our smooth flagstones.

Dad is dishing up, and it smells delicious.

'I forgot to have lunch,' he says, 'so this is kind of my lunch-supper. Like brunch, only in the afternoon.'

'It smells amazing,' I tell him. 'Just like Mae's mum made.'

'There's lots too,' he says. 'So we can have seconds.'

I laugh. I can't believe the way he's behaving. He's like a different person. He's not looking at me in that anxious way, in that 'have I done something wrong?' way. He looks like he's having a good time. Not mad, crazy good, just . . . normal good. He looks *relaxed.*

The knot of fear inside me relaxes a little too. 'Are you okay, Dad?'

He nods in between shovelling food into his mouth. 'I'm all right. I feel quite good today. Must be the drugs kicking in at last.'

The doctor gave him some tablets about a month ago, and they did tell him they'd take a while to work. Is this the answer then? Medicine? Has it fixed him? Will he be all right now?

The dinner tastes just as good as it smells, and I eat and eat, feeling warmth spread right through me.

'This is great, Dad! You can really cook!'

He looks pleased. 'I just followed the recipe. It's not that difficult.'

'Well, I think it's even better than Mae's mum

made it.' This isn't strictly true. There are some bits of rice that have clumped together, and one side of my chicken piece is a bit burned, but I don't say that. 'What are you going to make next?'

'I was looking through one of Coral's recipe books,' he says, and I jump slightly, since I can't remember the last time he used her first name. 'There's a beef casserole that looks nice. I might go shopping tomorrow.'

I beam at him. 'I can help if you like. Chopping vegetables or something.'

'Thank you.' He looks at me. 'How are you?'

'I'm good,' I say. 'I'm really good.' Because, for that moment, I am.

He smiles back. 'So am I. Chin-chin.'

We clink forks.

My heart is as full as my stomach. I want to freeze this moment in time so that I can find it again when I need it.

And it turns out I need it only two days later, when everything goes wrong again.

31

I come home from school on Thursday feeling happy. Mae and I are writing a Christmas story for the school newsletter. We told Miss Spotlin we were writing a book together (even though *After Armageddon* hasn't really got much further since we had the bad review) and she suggested we should write a Christmas one. And then she got all excited and said they could put it in the school newsletter.

'Actually,' said Mae afterwards, 'if it was long enough, they could print copies and sell them to raise money for the school. Like a fundraiser.'

Mae is always thinking of ways to raise money. I expect she'll be an entrepreneur when she grows up.

So as I walk down the road from the bus stop, I have a smile on my face and a warm feeling in my tummy. Mae and I have already decided what our story will be about. It'll be set in the First

World War and it'll be about a boy trying to get his dad home from the Front in time for Christmas. It will be uplifting and heartwarming and will make people cry. The very idea has already made Mae cry, so that's a good start.

I'm surprised that the light in the kitchen isn't on when I get in. Dad had been planning to make some kind of pie, but there's no smell of cooking, and nothing in the oven. In fact, the house seems quite dark and quiet. A small finger of fear pokes me, and suddenly I'm remembering Lisiella's mother, who gets very happy and then gets very sad and wants to die.

'Hello?' I call, my breath filling my chest too much so that it's hard to breathe out. 'Dad, are you here?'

There's no answer. I go into the library. The books we saved are neatly ordered on the shelves. He's not here. The lamp isn't on, but blue light spills from the computer screen. I go over to the desk and jog the mouse to clear the screensaver.

The email program is open. I hesitate. I shouldn't go nosing about in his emails. They're private. But my eyes can't help flicking across the screen, and once I've seen that there's an email titled *A History of the Lemon – submission response* I can't look away. I click on the subject title, and the email opens.

> *Thank you for sending us* A History of the Lemon. *It is undoubtedly the result of many hours of work, and we can see that it is thorough and expressive. However, the non-fiction market is very tough at the moment and we are sorry to say that we won't be taking on your book. We wish you luck in placing it elsewhere.*

Oh no. My heart drops into my stomach. I close the email and see that immediately underneath it is another, from a different publisher. The words are brisk and businesslike:

> *We regret that* A History of the Lemon *is not suitable for our list at this time . . .*

Two rejections. Two rejections of his life's work, coming within minutes of each other on the same day.

Where is he?

I run through the house, shouting for him. He's not in the kitchen. He's not upstairs, in his bedroom or mine, or my library, or the bathroom. I am relieved that he hasn't drowned himself in the bath. But has he gassed himself in the car? I run down the stairs so fast that I take the last three in one jump, and I throw open the door and slip along the paving to our dilapidated garage. The car is in there, but it is cold and empty.

My breath comes in uneven gasps as I look around wildly. Where could he have gone?

Has he left me?

I should ring someone. The police? But I can't bring myself to dial 999. It's not a proper emergency, is it?

I go back into the house. The phone is in the hallway, on a rickety shelf that comes away from the wall if you put too much weight on it.

I pick up the phone, ready to dial Mae's house. Her mum will know what to do. Or should I ring Antonia? I hesitate.

There's a very faint noise, so faint that I'm not even sure I've heard it. It's coming from the sitting room – Mum's room.

Suddenly I'm cold with fear. My back tingles

with apprehension. I push the door open, phone gripped tightly in one hand. I didn't look in here. I didn't even think of it.

It's dark. I've seen enough scary things on TV to know to switch on the light. My imagination is running riot. Is Dad bound and gagged on the floor?

When the light comes on I see him immediately. He's sitting on the sofa, staring at the empty fireplace. He's as still as a statue, just staring and staring.

'Dad?' I say. He's so still I wonder if he's paralysed. Maybe he can't actually move? Maybe he's been hit by some mystery illness and he's been stuck here all day, unable to call for help.

I go to sit next to him, still holding the phone. 'Dad. It's me, Calypso. Are you all right?'

He blinks, and some emotion flickers across his face. But he doesn't speak or turn his head.

'Do you need a doctor?' I ask. 'Can you move? Dad – I need you to speak to me.'

He licks his lips, as though they're too dry to form words. 'My book,' he says quietly.

'Oh, Dad. I know. I saw the emails. I'm so sorry.'

'Two in one day.'

'But that doesn't mean the others will reject it

too. You sent it to lots of publishers, didn't you?'

He remains silent.

'And anyway,' I plough on, 'lots of books get rejected to start with. *Harry Potter* did.'

This doesn't cheer him up. 'Years of work,' he says.

'I know. I'm sorry, Dad.' I put my hand on his arm and give it a squeeze.

He hardly seems to hear me. 'What will I do if no one wants it?' he says.

I don't know how to answer. 'Come on, Dad,' I say, pulling at his arm. 'Let's go and cook something nice for supper.'

But he won't move. 'I'm not hungry.'

I gaze at him, wondering what to do. In the end, I go and heat up some soup from a tin and bring it with a loaf of bread into the sitting room. It feels chilly in here, so I put some newspaper twists into the fireplace and add two logs on top. By the time I've found the matches and lit the fire, the soup is cold and he hasn't touched it.

'That's better,' I say, trying to be cheerful. 'A nice fire.'

It isn't a nice fire. I haven't made it very well, and it doesn't warm up the room at all. I blow on it in an attempt to make it spark up better. It spits pitifully.

I drink my cold soup and eat two slices of bread in silence. Dad is still immobile. Every now and then he says, 'My book,' like it's a missing child.

The fire goes out. I pick up our bowls and the bread and take them back to the kitchen. Then I wash up and put the kettle on. I'll make him a cup of tea. Maybe he'll drink it.

I make two mugs and carry them through. 'I've got to do my homework,' I tell him. 'Shall I bring it in here?'

I know he's heard me because he raises his eyebrows very slightly and makes an expression of 'I don't know'.

I bring in my school bag and sit on the floor. I talk to him while I do my homework. 'Miss Spotlin's given me a science sheet. I have to fill in these sections about magnets. Do you think the answer to number one is *a* or *b*?'

He doesn't reply, but somehow I keep going. Part of me, deep down, is growing very scared. He loves that book. He's been working on it for as long as I can remember. The lemons on the shelves were all part of it. What if no one will publish it? All that work . . . for nothing. No book. It would be even worse than the review for *After Armageddon*. That was just a small thing – this is big. Huge. His *magnum opus*. It's the most important thing in his life. More important than me, I think.

I want to batter down the doors of those publishers, scream in their faces. I want to write emails full of swear words, telling them what they've done. Don't they think of the person who's put their heart and soul into a book when they reject it? How can they write emails like that?

He's been making such an effort recently. He's really been trying to be a better dad. And things had been going so *well*! He was cooking! He was smiling, even laughing! I knew he had a long way to go still, but it was a beginning! I was starting to think we could be properly happy – and now *this*. What if he never recovers?

While my head fizzes with fear, I keep babbling about the questions in my homework. He sits, silent, occasionally sighing. I write nonsense for my answers.

When I finish, I take our mugs (his is still full) to the kitchen and put them on the side. Then I lean on the sink and stare out of the window at the blackness of the sky. What should I do? Should

I ring Antonia and tell her Dad's gone funny? But it's past six o'clock – she won't be at work.

I have this sudden aching desire to ring Mae. It is so strong it makes me tremble, and I have to hold onto the sink to stay upright. I don't want to do this on my own. Mae will help. Her mum will help.

But what if . . . what if Dad is crashing? Like Lisiella said? What if bringing other people in tips him over the edge? And if he tips over the edge, what will happen to me?

If Dad tries to . . .

If Dad . . .

Where would I go? Who would look after me?

I can't risk it. The best thing I can do is stay with him, keep close. Watch him. Be cheerful. Keep him going. Don't do anything different.

I look out of the window, at the indigo sky and its handful of pinpricks of light, and I take a breath.

Then I go back to the front room. One tiny orange spark glows faintly but the rest of the fire is dead. Determined, I rake out the ashes and build another fire, better this time. Girls like me used to build fires all the time when they worked as maids. It can't be that difficult.

When I have something resembling heat coming

from the pile of paper and wood I turn to Dad. He stares at the flickering light but otherwise hasn't moved at all.

'I'm going to get a blanket,' I say, 'and then we can watch the TV for a while. Okay?'

A very faint frown gathers over his eyes, as though he's trying to remember something, but he doesn't say anything, so I go upstairs and drag a big blue blanket out from under my bed.

There's a programme about the countryside on BBC Two. That will do. I put the blanket over his knees and curl up on the other half of the sofa. This room is almost cosy now. I begin to pretend that I am in a book. That helps. I am a poor girl, living with her invalid father, in Victorian Britain, with no prospects. But at the end of the book my rich aunt, who has been searching for me ever since her sister, my mother, died, will find me and we will live in luxury and warmth for ever more. A bit like *A Little Princess*, only without the India bit.

It's hard to imagine Victorian Britain when you're watching the television, though. And the programme starts talking about fox hunting, and there's a horrible bit with a mangled fox, and I glance sideways at Dad, wondering if I should change the channel. But he's staring at the screen like maybe he's interested. So instead, I close my eyes and go back to the story in my head.

After the countryside programme, there's a quiz. And then the news. Dad doesn't get up even to go to the toilet. We sit there for three hours, staring at the TV, and I write an entire novel in my head.

Eventually, I realise we're going to have to do something about going to bed. Can I leave him alone in his room? But what if . . .?

No. I can't. I'll have to spend the night in his room, somehow.

'Dad,' I say. 'It's time to go to bed.' I switch off the TV.

He comes, unresisting. Is that a good sign? Getting him up the stairs is hard work. I push him from behind, and he staggers up on all fours, like a child or a really old person. I make him go to the bathroom and stand outside anxiously. When he comes out I remind him to wash his hands, so he goes back in again.

I don't even try to make him take his clothes off. Instead, I tell him to sit down on his bed, and I remove his shoes. Then he lies down and I put the duvet over him.

‘Thanks, Calypso,’ he says, his gaze fixed on the ceiling. His eyes are wide open.

‘I’m going to sleep in here,’ I say. Then I go to my own room and drag the mattress off the bed. I’d never realised how heavy mattresses are – and it doesn’t have handles or anything to hold onto, so getting it across the landing and through Dad’s doorway is like hefting an elephant. By the time it thumps awkwardly to the floor of his room, I am sweating and dizzy.

I fetch my duvet and pillow and make up my bed on the floor. Then I go to the bathroom and do all the usual things. I’m getting into my nightie when I realise I should check that the front and back doors are properly locked. I put on my dressing gown, which is two sizes too small, and go back downstairs. The stone flags burn cold through the worn-out soles of my slippers.

The remains of the fire glow stubbornly. I wonder if I should put them out completely. Is there a risk that the house will catch fire if there are any embers left alight?

I am so tired I almost sob with the weight of having to make a decision. In the end, I leave the fire to put itself out and crawl back upstairs, my feet blocks of ice. If we can just get through tonight, maybe it will all be better in the morning.

I get under my duvet and rub my feet. Dad is completely silent. Is he breathing? I have to get up to check.

His eyes are still open, and as I sit up he whispers, 'All that work . . .'

I press my hand to my mouth so that I can't cry. Then I lie down again.

It's going to be a long night.

32

I don’t know how much I sleep. I keep waking up to check that Dad is still alive. You can’t die from sadness, can you? I know it can’t really be possible, but still I can’t help being frightened.

When it’s half past eight, I get up. I am pleased to see Dad is breathing even though his eyes are closed. I wonder what time he fell asleep. I tiptoe out of the room so as not to wake him.

It’s Friday, but I can’t go to school and leave him. I boot up Dad’s computer and write an email to the office: *I’m sorry to report that Calypso was sick last night, so she won’t be in today. Yours sincerely.* It’s lucky for me that the school accepts sick notes via email.

There are rules about sickness and school. You can’t go back until you’ve had two clear days of not being sick. If necessary, I can use the same excuse on Monday.

I listen to a programme about Anne Frank on Radio 4 while I eat some toast. It's really interesting and I try to remember some things to tell Mae later.

I call Antonia, but it goes to voicemail. I hesitate. I don't know what to say. 'Hi, it's Calypso. Um . . . I just wondered . . . Dad's a bit down. Er . . . maybe I'll talk to you on Monday.' I hang up, feeling stupid. I hate leaving messages. I never know what to say.

Looking for something comforting, I go into Dad's library, still in my nightie and dressing gown. The books that we managed to save take up less than half the shelf space. The rest of the shelves are empty. I feel a pang for the books that didn't make it, as though we turned off their life support. But they were the ones whose pages simply dropped out, the glue from the binding dissolved; the ones with mould so black that the paper was slimy with it.

I run my fingers over the spines of the books that have made it – the scarred survivors. I reach a hardback with a torn dust jacket and take it down. It's a copy of Charles Dickens's *Great Expectations*. I flick through it. The print is so small! How did people read it without getting a headache?

Mum's shelf is only half full now. I insisted her books went back on the same shelf they always lived on. *To Kill a Mockingbird* is absent. So are *Frederica*, *Jamaica Inn*, *The God of Small Things*, *The Bell Jar* and at least five others.

I reach for one that should really have been thrown away, but I couldn't bring myself to do it. It's *Jane Eyre* by Charlotte Brontë, and I wouldn't have saved it except . . .

On the flyleaf is my mother's handwriting, neat and careful as it is in all her books: *Coral Costello, aged 10½.*

The same age I am now.

My fingers tremble as I touch the writing. This is a little piece of her – Coral – when she was exactly my age. Coral the child, a long time before she became my mum.

Was this book one of her favourites? Not that it matters. I shall read it anyway, just as I shall read all of her books over time. I turn the pages, holding my breath. *Her* eyes followed these same words. The story flowed into her mind, just as it now flows into mine. Through this book, we are connected. And there she is again, in my mind's eye, smiling in the sunshine. Books give you more than stories. Books can give you back people you've lost.

I wish you were here, I think. I wish more than anything. I close my eyes, and wish and wish and wish so hard I think the wishing part of my mind might break.

33

Dad stays in bed. I take him food and drink, but he barely touches a thing. I know a person can go a long time without food, but it's important to drink water.

'You have to drink,' I tell him at midday. I hold the glass to his lips until he has to take a sip. Then I put his hands on the glass and tell him to hold it himself.

I try to cheer him up. I even read him a few pages from a book, but he closes his eyes and turns over, pulling the duvet up over his shoulders. I suggest he comes downstairs and we can watch TV together, but he doesn't say anything

Antonia doesn't ring back. I don't know why. Maybe the voicemail recorder is broken. Maybe she's not in the office today. Maybe she's off sick. Or maybe she listened to my message and thought it didn't sound important. *Is* it important? I don't know. I think about ringing her again, but I don't want to be a nuisance.

At the back of my mind is the nagging worry that if I tell someone, they might take me away from Dad. And if I'm not here to look after him, who knows what might happen?

I go back to Dad's library and take down *Jane Eyre*. The scene where she is taken to the red room makes me shiver in fear. Poor Jane! And she had lost *both* her parents. So many people in stories grieving for loved ones. In a way, it's kind of reassuring. I'm not the only one.

But as I read on, my brain starts firing on its own: new characters burst into my thoughts, clamouring to tell their own story. I abandon *Jane Eyre*, fetch some sheets of paper and a pen and lie on the floor. My pen flies across the paper, filling it with phrases and sentences that I hardly think about. It's like my brain is spilling words and ideas onto the page without letting me know what they are first. It feels like magic.

The house is still and quiet, but I don't mind it now, because my head is on fire, full of thoughts and dreams and memories, and I'm writing about my mother as she must have been as a child, and about a lonely boy who doesn't know how to make friends. And in my story they meet, and she fills his head with flowers and music and jokes and journeys, and the boy realises that being one of two is better than being one of one, and they decide they'll be together for ever because life is just better that way. A million, squillion times better.

34

When my arm aches so much that I can't actually hold the pen any more, and I have filled over twenty pages with writing, I rub my eyes and realise it must be well past six o'clock. The room is almost completely dark.

I scramble up, grabbing the sheets of paper. Dad! I have been so lost in my own world, he could have come down the stairs or run a bath, cooked a meal or . . . or *died*, and I wouldn't have heard. I'm supposed to be looking after him!

I run upstairs, taking them two at a time, panic and guilt flooding through me.

I push open his door and almost collapse with relief. He's not dead. He's actually sitting up in bed. The eyes that he turns on me are sad and tired, but at least he's looking at me.

'I'm so sorry,' I blurt out. 'I was writing downstairs,

and I lost track of time. Are you all right? I'll make you a cup of tea. And some toast.'

The skin between his eyebrows furrows, as if he's trying to understand me. 'Tea?' he says.

'Yes! Yes, tea. I'll make some, all right?'

'All right.'

I realise I am still clutching the scrawled-on papers. 'Oh – here. This is what I was doing.' I thrust them at him, but he moves so slowly to take them that I put them down on the bed, fidgeting. 'It's a story,' I say. 'You can read it if you like.'

'Thank you.' He stares down at the pile of crumpled paper.

I hesitate for a moment. 'They're probably all out of order,' I say. 'I'll sort them out for you.'

It takes me a few moments to tidy the sheets into a neat pile. 'There you are,' I say. 'I'll just go and make some tea.'

He is sitting up. The relief makes me light-headed as I walk to the kitchen. He's kind of slow to understand, but he's not doing that zombie thing any more, so that has to be a good thing, doesn't it?

I am slightly disappointed to find that he hasn't moved when I get back upstairs with the tea and a couple of biscuits. The pile of paper still sits neatly on the end of his bed, and he's still staring at it.

'Your tea,' I say, putting it down on the bedside table.

'Thank you.' He doesn't move his lips much, so it's hard to hear the words properly.

I'm not quite sure what to do. I feel frustrated and tired and keyed up and hungry all at the same time. I should probably have something to eat – I don't think I remember having lunch.

'Tomorrow's Saturday,' I say to Dad, perching on the end of the bed and moving my story closer to him. 'Less than two weeks till Christmas. I mean fewer. Fewer than two weeks. Shall we go Christmas shopping or something?' I know this is a silly thing to say. We don't have money for presents, do we? Or do we? I haven't had any pocket money for a long time. 'Well, we could go out and look at the shops anyway. They're full of decorations and things. There's one in the middle of town that has a whole animatronic nativity scene, Mae says.'

Dad nods slowly – so slowly that he looks almost animatronic himself. The thought makes me want to giggle. I swallow hastily.

Dad still sits in bed, staring with a look of faint puzzlement at the far wall.

On an impulse, I lean forward and take his hand in mine. 'Dad,' I say. 'Dad. Come back. You've gone somewhere. Come back to me.'

To my utter astonishment, his eyes fill with tears as he stares, unblinking, into space. And then he gently takes his hand away from mine and puts it in his lap.

I have to clamp my lips together very hard, because I have a terrible pain in my heart again. Is he deciding that he doesn't want to be with me any more? That maybe he doesn't want to live any more? I leave the room and stand on the landing, clutching the banister for support. What happened to his inner strength?

The phone rings downstairs. I don't know whether to answer it or not. Could it be Antonia? The only other person who'd be ringing at this time on a Friday evening is Mae. I want to talk to her so badly. But how can I? How can I tell either of them about Dad?

I wait. Eventually the phone stops ringing, and I want to cry because I feel so alone.

I think back to the day Mae held me while I

cried about Mum. It felt awful and wonderful at the same time. I didn't have inner strength that day, I just had Mae. *She* was my strength. I needed her.

And then I realise.

Dad doesn't need inner strength. He needs *me*.

35

The thought is like a bolt of lightning.

Dad needs me. This isn't just about me looking after him when he's depressed. This is about *us*, about how we exist, here, together.

How have I not understood it before? All this time, he's been acting like he doesn't need me, telling me that we are two independent people. But it's a lie!

Of *course* he needs me. Just like I need him, like I've always needed him – even more since Mum died. So why has he been pushing me away?

Mae is my friend and I need her. What would I do if I lost her?

Of course, that's it.

He didn't want to love me like he loved Mum, *because Mum died.* And when you love someone, losing them hurts so badly you almost wish you hadn't loved them in the first place.

And he's been telling me he doesn't need me in order to protect me. Trying to get me to build walls around my own heart so that I can't be hurt in the way he's been hurt.

But he's got all this so wrong. People need people. You can't just keep yourself apart all the time so that you don't get hurt. All that means is you get hurt anyway *and* you're alone.

The thoughts explode and collide in my head, and outside it's as though the world slows to settle into a new pattern.

Dad isn't alone. He's got me. And now I understand where to find my inner strength. It has to be *given* to you by other people. When someone cares about you, they give you a bit of themselves. It strengthens you. Mae's friendship has made my life more exciting, warmer, more colourful . . . *happier*. And I can tell, from the way she beams when she sees me, that I give her something worthwhile too. We are stronger together than we are apart.

I'm going to be there for Dad. I won't leave him.

I'll stay right by his side until he comes out of the crash, because I can give him the strength that he needs to get through this.

And afterwards, we will be stronger together than we have been apart.

36

It's Saturday morning, and the house feels quiet and peaceful. I sit in Dad's bedroom and read to him, then I go downstairs and write a new story. I even do a bit of cleaning. I can't remember the last time someone cleaned the bath taps. I'm surprised how much I like making them shine.

Mae rings in the afternoon.

'I'm fine,' I tell her. 'I felt sick yesterday, so Dad let me stay home from school.'

'I missed you,' she says. 'We made our own word-searches and gave them to each other. Mine was the hardest in the class and no one got all the words!'

I feel a twinge of envy. I'd have loved to do that.

'You'd have got all the words,' she says loyally. 'I've saved you a copy so you can have it on Monday.'

'Thanks,' I say, hoping so very much that Dad will be better then.

'Have you written your letter to Father Christmas?' Mae asks.

'No,' I say. 'I haven't done that for years.'

'Oh,' she says. 'Well, I did one. You never know, right?'

I smile. Mae is so romantic about that kind of thing. 'What did you ask for?'

'Books! And book tokens! And a bag that has pictures of books on it. And some new pens.'

'That's what I'd put on my list. And some notebooks, for new stories.'

'Oh no, notebooks! I forgot about them!' Mae sounds genuinely horrified.

I laugh. 'I'm sure someone will get you notebooks.'

'Are you coming for Christmas?' she urges. 'You are, aren't you?'

I hesitate. How long does a crash take? Dad can't leave the house in this state.

'Well,' I say, 'he hasn't actually said yes yet. But he will. I'm sure he will.' I cross my fingers and hope with all of my heart that I'm right.

I can almost hear her jogging on the spot.

'You have to come, you have to! I will come over and kidnap you if he says you can't!'

I laugh again. It's so good to laugh – it feels like days since I last laughed. 'You wouldn't need to! I'll run all the way to yours if I have to!'

'I really missed you yesterday,' she says again. 'I had to sit with Aaliya, and she kept trying to copy me. It was really annoying.'

I cradle the phone to my ear as she tells me more about school. I've only missed one day, but it feels like longer. Sitting in my silent house with Dad has made me realise how much I like being with other people. Especially Mae and her family.

But I still can't tell her what's really going on. I can't risk it. So when she says, 'Do you want to come round tomorrow?' I have to say no.

She sounds disappointed. 'But you're not feeling sick any more, are you?'

'No,' I say, 'but I might be infectious.'

'Oh.'

'I wouldn't want to pass on my germs,' I say, the lies falling easily from my lips. Inside, I feel twisted. I hate not telling her the truth.

On Sunday morning I have to hold back a gulp when I take Dad a mug of tea and see that he's actually reading my story. He is deep in concentration, his eyes sliding in neat tracks across the page. I watch him, fascinated, unable to look away and yet knowing how off-putting it is when someone watches you while you're reading. I make myself put down the mug on his bedside table, my ears almost throbbing from the effort of listening. Will he laugh? Or sigh? But he simply reads, his face a blank.

I close the door behind me in an agony of anticipation. I have to find something to do while he reads, otherwise I'll go mad listening at the door.

I go into my own room and stare at it. It's time for a change. With some effort, I drag the bed frame from one side of the room to the other. And then I take the clothes out of my chest of drawers and the drawers too, and drag the base to a different position. I go to put everything back in the drawers but hesitate. I have grown out of a lot of these. One by one, I go through my tops, trousers and skirts, putting aside any that are too small. The remaining pile is rather sorry-looking. But maybe I could give the other clothes to Mae's mum and she could take them apart and make some new ones? That way we wouldn't need to buy any. I stare closely at the seam of a top. Surely, you just cut through the stitching and then sew it together in a different way, right?

I'm sure we have a needle and thread in the house somewhere. Before I know it, I'm searching through the kitchen drawers for sewing equipment. And within another half an hour, four tops lie in pieces on my bedroom floor and I am busy drawing a diagram of how to piece them together to make a new one.

Then Dad appears in the doorway, which makes me jump in surprise.

'I'm going to have a bath,' he says, and disappears again.

Well!

I sit back on my heels for a moment and gaze out at the landing. Has he finished reading my story? What did he think? He didn't say anything about it!

But. He's going to have a bath. It's the first time he's got out of bed (apart from going to the toilet) since the crash.

I mustn't expect too much too soon.

This is a good sign.

37

On Monday morning, I get up at the usual time, taking a moment to remind myself that the reason my bedroom looks unfamiliar is because I moved everything round. It's the last week of school, but I'm not sure whether to put on my uniform. I tiptoe to Dad's door and listen. I can hear his steady breathing, so he must still be asleep. He hasn't said anything about my story, which is driving me crazy, but I've promised myself I won't ask. He'll tell me when he's ready. And after his bath yesterday, he got dressed and we sat downstairs for a while in the sitting room while I read a book. He stared into space, but it was a different space than his bedroom, so I'm taking that as Progress.

I go downstairs, wincing at the cold flagstones, and make him a cup of black tea. The milk has gone off, so one of us needs to go to the shop today.

I carry it back upstairs and push open his door. 'Morning!'

And then the breath catches in my throat, because the duvet is covered with sheets of paper. My sheets of paper – and also many, many new ones, covered with Dad's own handwriting. He's been *writing*. In the middle of the night. For hours, by the looks of things.

The mug trembles in my hand, slopping tea over the rim. Hastily, I put it down. What has he been writing? I am gripped with dread. What if it's all about lemons again?

I reach out a hand to the nearest piece, but Dad's eyes flicker open and I step back, almost guilty.

'Calypso,' he says sleepily. 'What time is it?'

'It's a quarter to eight,' I tell him, though I can't stop my gaze from straying to the sheets of paper. 'How are you?'

He sits up, rubbing his eyes. 'All right, I think. What day is it?'

'Monday.'

'Monday? Is it?' He seems confused. 'Are you sure?'

'Yes.' I bite my lip. Is he really confused? I mean, he's often not known what day it is in the past.

Should I be worried? 'But I'll stay home and look after you.'

He frowns. 'Is it the holidays?'

'No. No, it's school today. But . . .'

'You should go,' he says.

Right now, all I want to do is read what he's written.

'School is important,' he says.

'What about food?' I say. 'Will you make sure you have breakfast? And lunch? We need milk. Maybe I should come home at lunchtime.'

'No,' he says, almost irritably. 'I'm fine, Calypso. For goodness' sake, I'm a grown man. I think I can look after myself.'

My mouth falls open, and my eyes sting in shock. Doesn't he *know* what I've been doing for him over the past three days? Has he no idea how worried I've been? How ungrateful! I can't believe it!

'Fine,' I say shortly. 'I'll go and get dressed.'

Suddenly, I can't wait to get out of there. Forget the sheets of paper. I don't care what he's been waffling on about. I get dressed and eat my breakfast, each mouthful hard to swallow. I am so hurt I don't bother to go up to say goodbye. Instead, I pick up my bag and call up the stairs, 'I'm off now. Bye.'

There is no reply.

I slam the door behind me.

38

Mae and I have the biggest hug ever when we see each other in the school playground.

'I have missed you SO much,' she sighs.

'I missed you too.' And although I try to hold them back, tears suddenly stream down my face.

'What's the matter?' Mae gasps.

I shake my head. 'I lied to you.'

'What about?'

'I wasn't sick on Friday.' Once I've started talking, I can't stop. I tell her about Dad's crash, about his non-talking, about my sleeping on his floor, trying to keep him alive. And about his dismissal of me this morning, as though I didn't matter at all.

Mae stares in horror. 'Oh, Calypso! That sounds awful! Let me talk to my mum. You can come and stay with us.'

For a brief, blinding second, I am going to say

yes. Dad said he could cope on his own – so let him prove it! But even as I feel my mouth opening to respond, I am shaking my head.

'No,' I say, wiping my face. And then, more quietly, 'No, I can't. That thing – remember I told you about inner strength? Well, I get it now. It was you who showed me, really. That your inner strength isn't for *you* – it's for other people. He needs me. It's really important that I stay with him. I promised myself.'

'But you just told me he was really horrible to you this morning,' Mae objects.

'Yes, but . . . but that was just him pushing me away again,' I say, realising the truth as I say it. 'He's used to being alone. I have to show him that it's not good for us.'

The bell rings. Kids rush past us, uninterested.

'Look, it'll be all right,' I say. 'Lisiella at the young carers' group says everyone goes through a crash. He'll come out of it. And yesterday he was better than on Friday and Saturday.'

'Calypso! Mae!' Miss Spotlin is standing in the doorway, looking out across the playground. We're the last ones out here.

'Tell you later,' I say, grabbing her hand and pulling her in. 'I've got wordsearches to make.'

39

I don't know quite what to expect when I get home. I stand on the front doorstep for a moment before I push the key into the lock. I've had such a good day at school; it's been like a holiday. I almost don't want to go in. That deep-rooted fear tugs at me. I've been away all day. Has he coped? What will I find?

I take a breath and open the door.

From my right, in the front sitting room, there is music playing. I put down my bag and stand in the hallway for a moment. I don't know the piece of music, but it's something big and orchestral. The violins are soaring and the trumpets are punching out a fanfare, then everything explodes in a joyful melody.

Dad is standing in the middle of the sitting room with his eyes closed. His hands twitch as though he is conducting the invisible instruments, and there's a strange expression on his face: sort of happy and terribly sad at the same time. Like a pain that's almost good.

His eyes open and he jerks, startled. 'Calypso. I didn't hear you come in.'

'Sorry. Er – are you all right?'

He turns down the volume on the CD player. 'I'm listening to Elgar.'

'It's nice. Loud.'

He sinks into the sofa, as though he's suddenly unable to stand any more. 'I'm tired.'

'I know, Dad. Did you get some milk? Did you remember to have some lunch?'

He shakes his head. 'I'm not hungry.'

'*Dad.*' I put my bag on the floor. 'You have to eat. How can I go out and leave you if you can't look after yourself?'

He makes a sound like a snort. 'Don't be ridiculous.'

'I'm not, Dad. This is crazy. You have to eat.'

'Maybe *I'm* crazy,' he says, with an attempt at sarcasm.

A pang goes through me. 'Don't say that.'

There's a silence.

'I want us to go to Mae's for Christmas Day,' I blurt out.

'Oh, Calypso, not now.'

'Yes, now,' I say crossly. 'You keep putting it off, but they need to know. So they can order the right food and stuff. And it's the end of next week, Dad. What else are we going to do all day? Sit in silence and get depressed?'

He huffs. 'I didn't realise my company was so poor.'

'Can we go?'

'Are you asking me or telling me?' he snaps.

'I'm asking,' I say, feeling tears prick at my eyes. 'I just think it would be really nice.' Warm. Fun. Like a family.

He's got one hand clamped to his forehead, as though he has a pain, and he doesn't say anything else.

I sigh. The CD comes to an end and spins to a stop. I go over to switch off the machine, and then I see the pile of papers. My story – and the pages I saw this morning, sticking out from the bottom.

'What's this?' I dare to ask.

He doesn't answer.

It's half mine, so I reason that I'm allowed to

take it all. I go into the kitchen, the story clutched in my hand, fill the kettle and sit at the table to read.

My story was about a sad, lonely boy who had no friends and who met a girl who shone like the sun, and he realised that the world was a more amazing place because there was someone else to share it with.

Dad's story takes up where mine left off. His handwriting begins hesitantly at first, but by the end of the first page it is flowing and strong.

> *And the boy said to the girl, We shall be together for ever. And she smiled and took his hand and said, But of course. Because that is how life should be, sharing and exclaiming and crying and laughing together. And they went out into the garden, shouting and playing and throwing snowballs in the winter, and lying in the sun in July. And the boy felt as though he were no longer just one person. That somehow, the girl had become part of him, in his soul, his heart. And he loved her so much that even one minute away from her was too long.*

And they grew up together, and the girl helped the boy to enjoy being with people. She explained things to him and made him understand what other people felt and why they didn't always say what they meant or mean what they said. And the boy felt more and more confident and didn't mind going out to new places any more because the girl was by his side.

And then one day she said to him, Let's get married. And then we can do this for the rest of our lives. And he thought that at that moment he could never be any happier – but he was, on the day he saw her at the altar. She wore a white dress that made her look quite different, and for one panicky moment he thought she wasn't the same person. But then he saw the flowers in her hair and the crazy jewellery she wore that his mother always tutted about, and his heart turned over and he knew that despite the fancy dress and the nail polish and the make-up, she was still the girl he loved, underneath.

And his parents made faces like squeezed lemons and muttered that it would never last. And they were right – though not for the reasons they thought.

And the couple had a baby, and she was the light of both their lives, even though having a baby wasn't as easy or as fun as they had thought it would be. It was hard work, and often unrewarding, but then the baby smiled and laughed and learned to walk and to talk, and the sun shone more brightly than before. And the girl loved her baby so much that the love burst from her eyes and her hands, and the baby loved her mother too, running and calling to her at every possible moment. And the boy watched with some envy, because he knew he could never be so free and spontaneous, but he didn't need to be because the girl was.

And then they were parted. But not from lack of love, or from misunderstanding, or accident. From disease: a stealthy, creeping disease that had stalked the girl quietly for years. Biding its time, never showing its face, until it was too late and the doctors sighed and said they could do nothing.

And the baby didn't know where her mother had gone. She asked and asked until the boy couldn't bear to answer her, so he told her not to ask any more. And he took the pieces of his broken heart and locked them away, because he knew they could never be mended.

And then he began to turn himself into a monster. Because not only did he lock away his own heart, he taught the baby to lock away her heart too. He taught her that ideas and books were more important than people and feelings, and he watched with pride as she adapted herself to this solitary life, never realising that she was also lonely . . . and by then it was too late to say, I was wrong. I am sorry.

The words blur in front of me, but I have come to the end anyway. This is where Dad's writing stops. The end of his story.

I sit for a few minutes, letting the tears run down my face. And then I take up a pen and add:

But the baby discovered love and companionship all by herself, because the world isn't made for us to live in isolation. And then she taught her father to love again, because she knew that deep down, deep inside, he was still the boy who fell in love with the girl, all those years ago. And together they could bring the sunshine back and make him part of the world again.

And when I have finished, I wipe my eyes and pick up the extra page, and take it through to the front room to give to my father.

40

Antonia has left a message on the answerphone, telling me to call her if I need to. But by the time I pick up the message, it's past six o'clock and she wouldn't be in the office anyway.

I'm supposed to be going to the last young carers' group meeting before Christmas, but I don't want to remind Dad to take me. Things feel fragile, like we're on the edge of something, as though one wrong move could send us toppling over the cliff, but if I just say or do the right thing at the right moment, I might be able to drag us back to safety.

Dad reads the page I've written. And then he cries. It's so unexpected that for a moment I'm not sure what to do. But I go over and put my arms around him and say, 'It's okay, Dad. It's going to be okay.'

He cries stiffly, like he's rusty at it. And it isn't

long before he pushes me away (not in a mean way, though) and says, 'That's enough of that.'

It doesn't magically change anything. He goes back to bed and only eats a piece of toast for tea. But I feel like it's a small step.

A journey is made up of small steps, isn't it? And sometimes you need to sit down, or go back a bit because moving forwards is too scary, or there's something else you need to do first. But you can't go on a journey without small steps.

I know now that taking steps is a lot nicer and easier when there's someone to hold your hand. So I ring Mae and tell her how important she is to me. That she's made everything brighter and richer, and she's shown me shared wonder and happiness. And she cries, because Mae cries at everything – and that's okay, because it's happy crying.

And then I tell her we're coming for Christmas.

41

Mae practically squeals the place down when she opens the door on Christmas morning.

'Happy Christmas!' She brandishes a large red pillowcase at me. 'I've waited for you and it's been *agony*!'

'That's not a stocking!' I exclaim. 'That's a pillowcase!'

I feel ashamed of my own stocking – one of Dad's old knee-length socks, with tinsel sewn round the top. It's stuffed to bursting, but I can see presents peeping out of Mae's pillowcase that would never in a million years fit into my sock.

Mae takes my hand. 'Hey,' she says, 'I told you I'd share them, didn't I? Come on, we'll open them together. Oh! Is that the top you made?'

'Yes,' I admit. 'It's not very good. The seams are coming apart and –'

'I love it!' she exclaims. 'Turn around, let me see.'

I do so, self-consciously. It's made out of the four tops that I took apart. Mae's mum gave me a few tips, but I did all the sewing myself, which is why I'd rather no one looked at it too closely.

Mae says with admiration, 'That's really clever, Calypso. Can you make something for me?'

I laugh. 'Not until I've had some lessons from your mum!'

'You've done a wonderful job,' says Mae's mum. Then she smiles over my head at my dad. 'Happy Christmas.'

'Happy Christmas,' Dad says, handing over a bottle of wine. He still looks very tired, but he does try to smile back. 'Thanks for inviting us.'

'Come on into the warm,' she says. 'Today is about being comfortable. So don't feel you have to make small talk if you don't want to.'

'Oh,' says Dad. 'Oh – well, thank you.'

Mae's dad passes him a glass of spiced punch and asks him if he knows anything about Greece, since they're planning a holiday next year. As it happens, Dad does know quite a lot about Greece, so he immediately starts on a list of its best historical sites.

'*Stockings!*' says Mae, almost hysterical.

I rush to the sitting room with her. Christopher is already there, lying on the floor and playing with a new computer tablet. One finger is stuck up his nose as usual.

'Happy Christmas,' I say to him.

He says, 'Yeah,' and doesn't take his eyes off the screen. It makes me laugh.

Mae's house smells of cinnamon and oranges. There are candles on the mantelpiece and ivy over the mirror. A huge Christmas tree stands in the corner of the room. It's not a real one, but it's decorated with beautiful silver and blue baubles and lights, and tiny sparkling snowflakes.

We have a tree at home too, a real one, and Dad brought out our string of ancient lights, which are shaped like candles. We don't have many decorations, but getting them out year after year is like seeing old friends. We have a big box of paper streamers. They must be about forty years old and they're not very bright colours any more, but we still like them. You have to unroll them very carefully from the middle, so that they come out with twists in them. Rolling them up again after the New Year takes hours.

Decorating the house this year felt strange. Dad

wasn't sure he wanted to, but I made him. And he agreed afterwards that the house did look better with the streamers up, even though they made him cry a bit. He seems to cry a bit at all kinds of things now. It freaked me out to start with, but I don't worry now. In a way, it's quite reassuring.

He's had four rejections now for his History, and each one hurts, but I've told him that I'll help him to put it online so that people can still read and enjoy it, and that way all his hard work won't have been for nothing.

Antonia came round the day after her phone message. I told her about the crash, and she said she was sorry no one had got back to me on the Friday. One of her children was ill, and she'd had to stay at home to look after him. I was surprised; I hadn't even imagined that she had children. She told Dad he was making really good progress and she told me she was proud of me for handling everything so well. 'Though next time,' she added, 'don't go through it on your own, okay?'

I nodded and promised. Though I'm hoping there won't be a next time. It was nice to see her, and she gave me a big hug before leaving to deal with a crisis somewhere else.

'You first,' says Mae.

Mae's presents are much more exciting than mine, but she's very kind. She lets me have a beautiful notebook and a shiny gold pen from her hoard, as well as a chocolate snowman because there are two.

'I think Father Christmas knew I was going to share with you,' says Mae with a twinkle.

'Not Father Christmas,' I say. 'Your –'

'Shh!' she says. 'Don't spoil the magic!'

Christopher, still glued to his tablet, gives a loud snort. 'How old ARE you?' he says sarcastically.

Mae ignores him. 'I can't believe you're actually here today,' she says. 'I hoped and hoped so much, but I don't think I ever believed you would actually come.'

I smile at her. 'I can't believe it either. It feels like a dream. The best dream ever.'

Mae's mum comes in with warm, spicy drinks for us and we show her our stocking presents.

'You look beautiful,' I say, a bit shyly. She's wearing the skirt she made, and it shines in the fairy lights. Her hair is all swept up on top of her head and held in place with a big diamond-style clip. She looks like a film star.

Mae's mum looks surprised – and then she gives me a warm smile. 'Thank you, Calypso, that's a very kind thing to say. Why don't I start teaching you how to use the sewing machine in the New Year? You've got a good eye – I could teach you some simple techniques and you could make all kinds of things.'

I blush. 'I'd love that.'

'I like what you've done with your hair,' Mae says to me.

I touch the plaits that I've carefully pinned to my head. It took me half an hour to wrestle my springy red curls into plaits. 'I wanted to wear it like this because it was how you had your hair on the day we first met.'

'Was it? Wow, I don't remember that.' Mae grins. 'Feels like a long time ago now.'

'Yes, it does. Like years.'

We smile at each other.

Mae's mum glances at Christopher. 'We've set a timer on that tablet, you know. No more than two hours a day.'

'*What?*' he says, horrified. 'That's so unfair!'

'Screens are bad for you,' says Mae's mum smoothly. 'Your father set the time.'

‘Two hours is no way enough!’ complains Christopher.

Mae and I exchange glances. It may be Christmas Day, but families are still the same, aren’t they?

42

We go to church at ten and sing carols loudly. Then we come back to Mae's house and have the most enormous lunch I've ever seen. There's turkey and cranberry sauce and Brussels sprouts and roast parsnips and roast potatoes and peas followed by Christmas pudding and custard. Mae's dad switches all the lights off and then sets light to the pudding. We all gasp at the blue flame that floats around the dome before disappearing.

After lunch there are presents. I wasn't expecting much, but Mae's parents have bought me a brand-new pair of boots – knee-high brown leather with fur at the top. They are exactly the right size. I don't know what to say. I've never had boots like these, and I know instantly that I'll never want to take them off.

They've bought a present for Dad too – a new cookery book and oven gloves.

His expression softens. 'Duck with plums!' he says, turning the pages. 'Beef stew with stout and prunes! There's a nice recipe here for chicken with lemons . . .' And then his eyes widen as he realises what he's said.

Lemons.

The breath stops in my throat for a moment. I can feel everyone around me holding their breath too. How could he say it out loud? I still dream about that day. Mae lets out a tiny gasp and stares at me.

I feel as though everyone is waiting for my reaction. And for that time-frozen moment, I know I have a choice.

They're just lemons. Yellow fruit. We can't go around avoiding them for ever, can we?

I let out my breath very carefully. Then I take a new one, and straighten, and stretch my mouth into a smile. 'That sounds nice,' I say, and look Dad full in the face.

His gaze is uncertain, but he nods, and he tries to smile too, and then everyone around us relaxes, and Christopher starts another argument with his dad about the tablet.

The danger has passed. Or is it me who has passed a test?

Mae has made me a beautiful pencil case with a zip and everything.

'Mum did that bit,' she says, 'but I decorated it myself.'

The fabric is decorated with hundreds of tiny swirls and patterns, just like the ones on her wall. I give her a big hug.

I have made her a canvas collage, using copies of the front covers of all her favourite books. I got the idea from the activity we did at the young carers' group. Miss Spotlin helped me print out the covers on the computer one day after school and I cut them all out and stuck them onto a big canvas. Then I brushed varnish over the whole thing to make it shiny.

Mae bursts into tears when she sees it. It makes me laugh because I know it means she loves it.

'Do you hate it?' I tease.

'No, no, I love it!' she sobs. 'This is the best present anyone's ever given me!'

She's so funny.

'I have one more for you, Calypso,' says Mae's mum.

It's a bag made out of the leftover fabric from her skirt. It's the most beautiful thing I've ever owned. I love it so much that I am left speechless.

'Calypso,' says my father, 'don't be rude. Say thank you.'

'Ah, don't worry,' says Mae's mum, putting a hand on Dad's shoulder. 'She is saying thank you – look, with her eyes.'

After presents, there is a film on the TV and then food again – Christmas cake and chocolate yule log and tea and hot milk.

It's been the best day of my life, and although I don't want it to end, I don't mind going home again. In fact, part of me is longing for the peace and quiet of my own house. It's just me and Dad there, and although that's not easy now, it's familiar. Familiar family. I think maybe you can be a family with just two people.

One step at a time on our journey. But hopefully we're going the same way now. And soon, smiles won't be an effort, and maybe there'll be hugs. There's already more sharing. That's a good start.

When we're all stuffed and sleepy, I catch Dad's eye. He knows, because despite what he did to protect me, despite the difficulties we've had, he knows me better than anyone.

'Shall we go home, Calypso?' he says.

'Yes,' I say. 'Yes please. I think it's time.'

Epilogue

There's a scent of roses in the air, and as I sit with my pen flying across the paper a tendril of breeze creeps in through the open window of the writing den and tickles my neck. I barely notice because I am deep inside a story – a new one, a shiny bright idea that came to me only last night, just begging to be written.

I told Mae about it as soon as Dad and I got to her house, and she completely understood, so we went immediately to the den and that's where we've been for the past hour, her in one corner, me in another, both writing busily in our notebooks. At some point someone passed me a lemonade, and I think I must have drunk it, because the glass is empty, but I don't remember doing so.

It's a Saturday afternoon in the summer holidays, and Dad is in the garden with Mae's parents.

They're designing a new rock garden, but it mainly seems to involve sitting on sun loungers and looking at garden catalogues. Christopher is digging a fire pit. I don't know why and no one has asked him.

I can hardly believe that soon it will be the first-year anniversary of the day Mae and I met. So much has happened in all that time – too much to write in a book, at any rate. Perhaps one day, when I am old, I will write my memoirs – or maybe I should start earlier, before I get too forgetful. Because it would be awful to forget this moment: this space in time that is peace and quiet and warmth and imagination and writing and family and roses.

A bee buzzes lazily in through the window and lands on a page of writing in my book. It is fat and furry and glints in the sunlight, as though some of its hairs are made of gold. It makes me think of the story of Midas, the king who was cursed with the power to turn things into gold by touch. That makes me wonder what other kinds of powers you could have that would seem amazing to start with and then turn dark and deadly . . . and that sparks another brand-new shiny idea, begging to be written.

But I can't. I am deep inside this one, a story of accidental magic and fast friendships, so I write a few words to remind me of the new idea at the back of my notebook.

Mae yawns and stretches, straightening out her hand as though it has cramp. 'I've got stuck,' she says.

'It's writer's block,' I say understandingly. 'You need to do something else for a bit and then come back to it fresh.'

I've been reading a lot of books about the skill of writing recently. If writing is going to be my future career, then it's time I treated it in a professional manner.

Mae nods. Strands of her treacle-black hair are stuck to her forehead and she peels them away. 'I think the heat is making my thoughts slow. Are you going to take a break too?'

I hesitate. I am in a good part of a scene right now, and I don't really want to leave it, but it will wait because I know exactly what needs to come next.

'All right,' I say, and nudge the bee off my notebook. As it grudgingly hums away, I realise it has left a smear of pollen on the word it occupied on the page. 'Happy' now looks as though it's underlined in yellow. It makes me smile.

We go out into the fresher air and demand more lemonade from the grown-ups. Dad tuts for a moment, and then catches my eye and hastily agrees. He'll always be Dad, pernickety about words and manners and taking everything just a bit too seriously. But he smiles more than he ever used to now, and although there are days when his eyes darken and he turns away and has to be quiet and sad on his own somewhere, it doesn't scare me in the way that it did. He and Mae's dad are proper friends now, which makes me very happy.

I start a new school in September, but I'm not in the least nervous about it, because Mae will be there too. And then we're all going on holiday to Cornwall together in the October half term. Mae and I can't stop talking about it! We want to search for mermaids and dragons. If we don't find them, it won't matter because we can use the visit for research for a new series we're working on. I might even try to paint while we're there.

Dad bought me some oil paints for my eleventh birthday, and when I unscrewed the lid of one it made me cry because it smelled exactly like my library upstairs, the one that used to be Mum's studio. Dad said he was sorry for upsetting me, but it was the opposite, really. I was happy-crying, like Mae does. It was almost as though he was saying sorry for what he did to Mum's old books, by giving me something new that connects me to her.

Christopher lets out a yell as he accidentally thumps his own hand with the trowel, and Mae's mum rushes over, telling him off for being careless while making sure he really is all right. I've only recently realised that people do that a lot: say or do one thing in order to cover up a completely different feeling. I did it myself until I met Mae. Now I try to be truer to myself, because if you can't be true to yourself, how can you be true to anyone else?

If I don't become a writer, I might become a psychologist. People are a lot more interesting than I thought, and when you start to peel back their layers you find surprising things. I always thought inner strength was something you had to find for yourself. Now I know that the people who are strongest are the ones who love others and let themselves be loved back. There's a poem that says 'No man is an island', and I think I understand what it means. If you have inner strength but no one to love, what is it for?

Christopher is placated with a gel pack from the fridge and another lemonade.

'Lemon slice, please,' he says, holding out his glass.

Dad cuts into a fresh lemon, one he's grown himself, and plops the thick slice into Christopher's glass.

'Lemon for you?' Dad asks me, though he knows what I'm going to say.

I smile. 'No thanks.'

'Cricket!' shouts Christopher, waving a bat in the air.

Mae's mum takes a lot of persuading, but we get the stumps set up and Dad goes in to bat, and Mae drops the ball by mistake and everyone shouts at her, and then we laugh and Christopher bowls Dad clean out.

And the sun shines and the sliced lemon glistens in the light – and things are going to be all right.

Jo Cotterill

Jo Cotterill has had several careers – actor, musician, teacher, newspaper seller – but is now a full-time writer in Oxfordshire. She loves writing for all ages and has published over twenty books – the latest, *Electrigirl*, is about a superhero twelve-year-old and is part novel, part comic strip. Jo has previously been nominated for the Carnegie, shortlisted for the UKLA Book Awards and Highly Commended in the Oxfordshire Book Awards for her novel *Looking at the Stars*, a story about refugees and the power of the imagination. Jo loves going into schools to talk about books and reading, and can be found making cards or writing music when she's not spending time with her husband and two young daughters. Find her online at www.jocotterill.com or on Twitter @jocotterillbook.